NEON'S
SECRET
UNIVERSE

Books by Sibéal Pounder

Neon's Secret UNIverse

Tinsel: The Girls Who Invented Christmas

Bad Mermaids
Bad Mermaids: On the Rocks
Bad Mermaids: On Thin Ice
Bad Mermaids Meet the Sushi Sisters
Bad Mermaids Meet the Witches (for World Book Day)

Witch Wars
Witch Switch
Witch Watch
Witch Glitch
Witch Snitch
Witch Tricks

Beyond Platform 13 (with Eva Ibbotson)

NEON'S SECRET UNIVERSE

SIBÉAL POUNDER

Illustrated by *Sarah Warburton*

BLOOMSBURY
CHILDREN'S BOOKS
LONDON   OXFORD   NEW YORK   NEW DELHI   SYDNEY

BLOOMSBURY CHILDREN'S BOOKS
Bloomsbury Publishing Plc
50 Bedford Square, London WC1B 3DP, UK
29 Earlsfort Terrace, Dublin 2, Ireland

BLOOMSBURY, BLOOMSBURY CHILDREN'S BOOKS
and the Diana logo are trademarks of Bloomsbury Publishing Plc

First published in Great Britain in 2022 by Bloomsbury Publishing Plc

A catalogue record for this book is available from the British Library

ISBN: PB: 978-1-4088-9414-9; eBook: 978-1-4088-9413-2

2 4 6 8 10 9 7 5 3 1

Typeset by RefineCatch Limited, Bungay, Suffolk
Printed and bound in Great Britain by CPI Group (UK) Ltd, Croydon CR0 4YY

To find out more about our authors and books visit www.bloomsbury.com
and sign up for our newsletters

For Bella and Eddie. Thank you for helping me write this book at Tommy and Camille's wedding!

My Name Is Neon Gallup and I Just Wanted to Say!

Everything you've been told about unicorns is a lie! UNICORNS ARE NOT HORSES WITH HORNS!

Almost no humans know this, and I shouldn't even be writing it down.

They don't have hooves, or manes, or particularly magical names. Unicorns, *real* unicorns, look nothing like horses. Unicorns LOOK JUST LIKE YOU AND ME. It's almost impossible to spot one unless you know what to look for. They are the most magical beings on the planet – more magical than witches and mermaids and elves – and much more hidden. They live in a parallel world to ours and they call it the UNIverse.

Getting to the UNIverse is almost impossible, unless you find a way in.

But if you do ever manage to open a portal to the UNIverse, life will never be the same again …

1

Welcome to Brunty!

October, 1996
Three days until Neon's tenth birthday

Neon Gallup was on a quest to be normal.

Even though her family had moved from place to place all her life, and Neon had met *hundreds* of people, not a single one of them had ever considered her normal. She was always the weird one! But *this* time would be different.

Since they were moving to a new town, Neon decided it was the perfect time for a reinvention – to make her as normal as possible. She started with her clothes, ditching her favourite colourful, sequined and glittery outfits in favour of black everything instead. You couldn't go wrong with black, she decided. Every item of clothing she owned that wasn't black she had managed to dye before her parents had bundled her into the car. She'd kept her favourite tie-dye tights though.

'Look at the beautiful countryside, Neon!' Her father was smiling, almost desperately, as he drove them to their new life. Neon could tell he didn't support her efforts to blend in. Neither did her mother – who was fast asleep in the back, snoring loudly.

'Neon,' her dad prompted again. 'Look at the spectacular rolling hills!'

'I don't like green any more,' Neon said. 'It's the colour of celery, the *weakest* vegetable.'

'This is a very strange phase, Neon.'

'It's not a phase,' she informed her dad. 'You and Mum are making me move across the world, so I thought what better time for a reinvention.'

'Moving from Paris to Brunty is hardly across the world. You could fly it in a few hours. Is this *reinvention* the reason you've worn only black for the past week?' her dad asked tentatively.

'It's because I'm older and more sophisticated now.'

'Maybe you should also change your name, if you don't like bright colours any more,' he joked.

'Oh, I plan to,' Neon said. 'I'm thinking something snappy, like GLOOM.'

Her dad smiled. 'I know you don't mean that.'

'Only because I wouldn't know how to change my name,' Neon said.

They bumped along the road in silence for a few minutes.

'Have you thought of a name for the new cafe yet?' she asked.

Her dad's face brightened. '*Oh yes*. We're going to call it Ratty's.'

Neon looked up at him with a raised eyebrow. 'As in *rats*?'

'Yes,' he said, pointing to the back seat, where four very large cuddly toy rats were squished and seat-belted in beside her mum.

'I was inspired by your mother's genius,' Neon's dad said proudly.

Her mum was an artist, and one of her most popular

creations, much to Neon's horror, was human-sized cuddly toy rats.

'Ratty's,' her dad said grandly, sweeping a hand in front of him as if he were imagining the sign. 'The cafe that celebrates rodents!'

'You can't do that,' Neon said quickly. 'You'll never have any customers –normal people don't like rats!'

'All the more reason to do it – we can change their minds,' he replied. 'IT'S ABOUT TIME SOMEONE WAS NICE ABOUT RATS!'

Neon stared at him in disbelief.

'And if anyone comes in to dine alone,' he went on, 'I'll pop one of your mother's large rats in the seat opposite to keep them company!'

They passed the welcome sign for Brunty, their new home. Neon groaned as they trundled through the town, past little ramshackle shops and wonky stone walls.

'Isn't it lovely?' her dad said as they stopped at the traffic lights. 'Your mother used to holiday here as a child.'

But Neon was no longer paying attention, because on the patch of grass next to them, a group of people in matching tie-dye T-shirts were on their hands and knees, digging.

'Welcome to Brunty!' cried one of the strange people.

Neon stuck her head out of the window to get a better look.

'What are you digging for?' she asked.

'Oh, something *very* special! A treasure more precious than any other!'

Neon noticed their T-shirts had the words *The UH* stamped on them.

'What does that mean, *The UH*? Is it something to do with your search?'

'Oh yes ...' the woman said mysteriously, but before Neon could ask any more questions, the lights turned green and they were off.

'I wonder what all that digging was about?' Neon's mum said sleepily.

'Ah, you're awake,' Neon's dad said. 'Just in time!' He took a sharp right up a little hill and came to a stop. 'We're here!'

The hilltop was peppered with pretty stone cottages,

along with one very crumbly cottage and an even more crumbly cafe.

'Those two are ours. They need a bit of work,' he said. 'Oh, speaking of work – did we mention we'd like you to help us in the cafe for a while, Neon?'

'Just for the school holidays, until we hire some staff,' her mum added.

Neon put her head in her hands in despair.

Working at a cafe that celebrated rodents was not going to help her quest to be normal one little bit!

Inside the cottage, things got even worse: the new house was more cobwebs than house. There were holes in every floorboard and cracks in the ceiling.

'Why couldn't we move to an ordinary house?' Neon groaned.

'Oh, it's not too bad,' her mum said. 'Why don't you go and check out your room? It's got its own little bathroom, and you can see all the way into town from the window.'

So Neon plodded upstairs and plonked her box of

things on her dusty bed. She stood silently at the window, looking out across her new town.

'New town, new me,' she said, wiping the dust from the window sill. Underneath the dirt something caught her eye.

A unicorn, no bigger than a small coin, was carved into the wood.

'Weird,' she whispered, touching it lightly with her finger. Much to her surprise, the carving clicked and the window sill popped open like a box.

'A secret compartment!'

She lifted the window sill, plunged a hand inside and hit –

'SLIME!' she cried.

Sticky bits of sparkling, stretchy goo stuck to her hand.

'Ugh, bleurgh!' she gagged, as she waved her hand about, trying to shake it off.

There was something else in there, just beyond the goo. A little sliver of something poking out. Reluctantly, she squelched her hand back in and grabbed it.

It was a small and very old envelope, soaked in slime.

There was something lumpy inside it.

Neon wiped away the goo to reveal faded writing on the front.

SECRET!

DANGEROUS!

DO NOT TOUCH!

She shrugged and tipped the envelope upside down, excited to see what special treasure lay inside.

A dented and very old lipstick case fell out.

Her excitement slopped away like the slime. 'Why would anyone hide a lipstick?' she mumbled as she popped off the lid.

Luminous green lipstick.

A small sliver of paper was rolled into its lid. Neon unfurled it eagerly and read:

YOU NOW OWN THE RAREST OBJECT IN EXISTENCE! IN OUR WORLD, AND IN THEIRS ...

2

Ratty's

KNOCK, KNOCK, KNOCK.

'Neon!' her mum called.

'I'LL BE THERE IN A MINUTE!' Neon roared, leaping up and pasting herself against her bedroom door. Slime was splattered all over the floor!

The handle jiggled.

'BE THERE IN A MINUTE!' Neon said again, hoping her mum would go away. She'd never be able to explain the slime, and the secret compartment and the strange lipstick.

'I've left your Ratty's apron outside the door,' her mum called. 'We could really do with some help.'

Neon waited until she heard footsteps disappearing down the rickety stairs, then quickly and carefully placed the lipstick back where she'd found it and closed the secret compartment.

'I'll deal with you later, strange lipstick,' she said, pressing her forehead against the window in relief.

She did a double take. The view from the window had changed. Instead of the serene country scene, a terrifying sight of horror-film proportions came into focus! A girl dressed head to toe in pink with her hair pulled into bunches stood frozen on the driveway. Her hands were caked in mud.

The girl stared up at her, eyes unblinking.

The cryptic note flashed through Neon's mind: *Dangerous. Do Not Touch.*

Before Neon could scream, the girl burst into life.

'NEON GALLUP!' she yelled.

'It knows my name,' Neon whimpered.

'I'M PRISCILLA KNACKERMAN FROM NEXT DOOR! WELCOME TO BRUNTY!'

'Oh,' Neon said, practically collapsing with relief. She yanked the window open. 'What happened to your hands?'

'I WAS DIGGING. ANYWAY, SEE YOU AROUND!'

Neon watched the girl stalk up the drive and into the cottage next door.

'Digging? Why is everyone digging in this town?' Neon muttered as she went to the hallway to fetch her Ratty's apron. She groaned. It was brown and furry, with a large rat nose and whiskers on the front pocket.

Embarrassing, she thought. *Why can't we just have a normal cafe?!*

Neon's parents had wasted no time making Ratty's as weird as possible. When she walked into the cafe, her dad was slopping rat-brown paint on the walls. The brown tables had already been accessorised with lava lamps and the backs of the chairs were lined with glow sticks. And perched at each table was a human-sized cuddly toy rat wearing a glow-stick necklace.

Neon's mum was busy painting a Ratty's logo on the counter.

It was just the three of them, except for a man and woman nosily peering through the window. They were

14

wearing the same strange T-shirts as the people digging by the roadside.

'Ah, Neon!' her dad said cheerily. 'Why don't you take a Ratty's pad and pen, and a nice new menu, and see if the people at the window are potential customers?'

The people in the tie-dye T-shirts hastily shot off in opposite directions.

'I don't think they want a—' Neon scanned the menu. 'A RATPUCCINO. Oh please, you can't call the coffees ratpuccinos!'

'It's a very clever pun, Neon,' her dad said defensively. 'Just like my one for a latte – can you guess what it is?'

She smiled weakly. 'It's not a *ratte*, is it?'

Her dad beamed. 'Oh yes it is!'

'I think Ratty's is silly,' Neon said. 'Everyone is going to think I'm weird.'

Her dad's face fell and her mum dropped her paintbrush.

'I just want to be normal!' Neon cried.

3

No Way!

That night, Neon stared at the strange lipstick, popping the lid off and clicking it back into place. She sat like that for hours, until darkness fell and the whole town was asleep.

Why would someone hide an old lipstick? she wondered. And what exactly did the weird writing mean? *Dangerous? Their world?*

As she mulled over the possibilities, she began pacing up and down, dragging the lipstick along her bedroom wall as she went, creating a long and smudged line from one end to the other. She had decided to paint the wall black the next day anyway, so it didn't really matter.

She headed to her crumbly old bathroom to brush her teeth.

At first it wasn't obvious, but by the time the toothpaste hit her tongue, the bathroom had become strangely bright. Neon hummed as she brushed and lazily fiddled with the light switch, wondering if she'd turned on an extra light by mistake.

Within seconds it became very clear no light bulb was involved.

The edges of the bathroom door frame were ablaze with sparkling light.

Slowly, toothbrush firmly clamped in her mouth, Neon crept towards the door. She turned the handle and –

Flashes of colour were shooting around her bedroom! Fizzing stars crackled above her bed! Huge explosions of light came hurtling towards her, spraying glitter across the floor!

Her eyes grew wide when she saw where it was coming from.

'*Impossible*,' she whispered.

She dared to step closer.

The toothbrush fell from her mouth and hit the floor.

'No *way*,' she gasped. 'NO *WAY*!'

4

Into the UNIverse!

W here only moments earlier there had been a line of lipstick, there was now a huge rip in the wall, gushing rainbow light and dispensing unruly silver stars all over her bedroom. Neon desperately tried to patch up the hole, pulling and stretching it and pasting Spice Girls posters over it.

Nothing was working! She ducked as a star came hurtling towards her head and *pinged* off the wall.

The sounds of a busy street filled the room.

Nervously, she peered past the peeling wallpaper to what lay beyond. Her hair whipped about furiously in the wind as more streams of stars and glitter spilt out. She could see a town! She could see people! A huge crowd of them, getting bigger by the second! They were all staring at her. Some were pointing. A few were screaming. Everything was neon-coloured and it was giving her a headache.

'A rip!' someone from beyond cried. 'To the humans!'

'I thought they got rid of all the portal openers?'

Neon backed away from the wall.

'She's leaving!'

The crowd inched forward.

'She knows too much, what are we going to do?'

'Maybe someone should ask Greg …' one of them said with a sarcastic snort.

'We could capture her?'

Neon clenched her fists to stop herself from trembling.

'Look – you're scaring her!'

The crowd inched closer still.

'Aww, she looks quite sweet.'

'Well, we can't just leave her and hope she forgets! Every single unicorn life is now at stake!'

Neon picked up the lipstick and stared at the window sill. *Unicorn.* Did someone just say unicorn? She couldn't see any horsey creatures, just people with glittery, colourful hair and shimmering outfits.

'THE PORTAL WON'T CLOSE UNTIL SHE USES IT! SOMEONE DO SOMETHING!'

'Should we go and get her, or will she attack?'

'I think she looks nice.'

'You go and get her then if you're so sure she's nice.'

'I'm allergic to humans, so I can't.'

'You can't be allergic to humans!'

'Yes you can, and I am ... *ACHOO*!'

'What are the symptoms of being allergic to humans then?'

'It's ... um ... you sneeze and um ... get a rash ... an invisible rash. OH NO, I'M SO ITCHY EVEN THOUGH YOU CAN'T SEE A RASH!'

'You're such a liar.'

Neon crouched under the rip and thumbed the lipstick nervously as the people in the crowd prattled on. What was she going to do?

'She doesn't look like she's planning to step through any time soon, does she? She's trying to hide!'

'Maybe someone should go and nudge her in here.'

Neon began to crawl away from the rip and towards the door.

'I'LL NUDGE HER!' came a cry. 'MEEEEEE!'

Before Neon knew what was happening, a young girl came hurtling through the rip and landed face first on her bedroom floor with a horrendous *bang*.

'You let MOYA go and get her? *Moya?*'

'I hardly let her! She just … ran.'

Neon stared at the girl as she clambered to her feet. She was dressed in head-to-toe unicorn clothing – unicorn leggings, a unicorn jumper, even a unicorn head-band. And her trainers had rainbow manes instead of laces. Her blonde hair was

tied up and she had a streak of pink hair at the back of her head.

'I'm Moya McGlow!' the girl blurted out, bouncing excitedly on the spot. 'IT'S MY FIRST TIME MEETING A HUMAN AND OH WOW WHAT'S YOUR NAME AND TELL ME EVERYTHING ABOUT YOURSELF!'

'Erm, my name's Neon Gallup,' Neon replied awkwardly, unsure what to say at all. What did the girl mean, it was her first time meeting a human? The girl *was* a human … 'You, um, like unicorns I see,' Neon said, nodding at her outfit.

The girl looked confused for a moment and then laughed.

'Oh, you mean these weird horse-with-horn things – they're not *real* unicorns,' Moya said. 'They're Greg's unicorns. I'm a big fan of the *idea* though.'

Neon stared at her blankly. That was the second time she'd heard the name Greg.

'You've opened a portal, Neon. Everyone is freaking out because it's been ages since a portal has opened to the human world like this. This is a big day!'

24

'I opened it with this lipstick. Someone had hidden it in the window sill …' Neon trailed off.

'Not to worry. It's been a mystery for ages – us unicorns have searched for that portal opener for years.' Moya nodded at the lipstick. 'You've just found the last one on Earth.'

'You mean, *you're* a unicorn?' Neon said in amazement.

'That's right.'

'But you don't look like a unicorn.'

'Um, it's a bit hard to explain,' Moya said. 'But if you come with me, it'll all make sense.'

Neon looked at the rip in the wall and tried to resist the urge to know more. Moya seemed perfectly nice, but the world she'd accidentally opened up could be dangerous. And even worse, the whole thing was WEIRD.

'Come on, let's go – you'll love it,' Moya said.

'I can't go in there with you,' Neon said.

Moya frowned. 'Why not?'

'Because I'm on a quest to be normal.'

'That doesn't sound like a very fun quest,' Moya said flatly.

'HURRY UP, MOYA!' came a shout from beyond the stars. 'I thought human kids were itching to discover hidden magical worlds!'

Moya shuffled closer and lowered her voice to a whisper. 'Maybe *you* could become a unicorn.'

Neon laughed. 'I don't want to be a unicorn! If you're a unicorn, I don't know how you're hiding your hooves or your mane or the sparkly horn on your head, but I don't want them!' The thought made her feel woozy.

Moya looked confused again. 'Obviously you won't have *those*. Like I said, those are *Greg's* unicorns. He just made them up to distract the humans. *Real* unicorns look like humans, but they're magic! We command goo and we are mighty!'

'Command goo?' Neon spluttered. 'What do you mean?'

'You know, *goo* – I'll show you. There's a goo for practically everything!' She gestured to the gigantic

26

unsightly rip in the wall. 'Come on, step into *the UNIverse* with me.'

'The UNIverse?' Neon said quietly. She felt the intrigue swirling around her. Or maybe it was the stars. *A unicorn?* she mused. *Command goo? Be mighty? Nah,* she decided, *not for me. I'd rather be norm—*

'TO THE UNIverse!' Moya cried, pushing Neon head first through the portal before she could finish her thought.

5

Lumino

Ten seconds later, Neon stood silently on the other side of the rip, squinting at the technicolour world in front of her. It was daytime in the UNIverse and it looked a lot like the human world, only brighter, like someone had come along and coloured everything in. Pink, green, yellow and orange clouds hung in the sky, and people wearing glittering outfits and sporting neon stripes of hair crowded her, whispering fast.

She turned back to see the almighty rip – and the view of her bedroom – was rapidly getting smaller.

'Wait, no!' Neon cried just as it vanished from sight. She felt the panic rising in her. How would she get home? She clutched the lipstick tighter.

It had better work both ways.

Just across the colourful street and beyond the even

more colourful crowd, she could see a grand purple shop sparkling brighter than all the others. Smartly dressed people were dribbling out of it and pooling around her excitedly.

'That purple shop is the Goomart!' Moya said cheerfully. 'We're in the capital city of the furthest corner of the UNIverse – it's called Lumino.'

'Lumino,' Neon whispered in awe.

'And over there is everyone's favourite cafe,' Moya went on. 'Glittervoles!'

Neon took it all in. Multicoloured glittering parasols provided shade for the glamorous diners at the tables outside. She inched closer – she was *sure* she saw a little rodent swimming in one of the customer's drinks!

'We can't go yet,' Moya said, pulling Neon back.

'Is there a rat in that glass?' Neon said, pointing at the diners.

'No, it's a vole,' Moya said casually, as if having a vole in your drink was completely normal. 'It's creating the fizz – it wouldn't be a Volefizz drink without it! Come on, before we do anything, we need to take you

to the Gooheads. They're in charge of the UNIverse and they'll want to see you.'

'The Gooheads?' Neon asked. 'Are they a family or something?'

'Um, well …' Moya said awkwardly. 'I suppose you could say that …'

6

Meet the Gooheads!

Neon and Moya marched along the multicoloured pavement until they reached a large, sparkling stone building. Above it, letters made with sloppy goo read: *GOOHEAD CENTRAL.*

Carved in shimmering rock next to the front doors was a statue of a smug-looking man with a strange haircut cuddling a unicorn – the fake horse kind. The *Greg* kind.

'That's Greg,' Moya said, nodding at the statue.

'What's wrong with his hair?' Neon asked. 'It's short on the top and long down the back.'

'Oh, haven't you seen a haircut like that before? It's called a MULLET,' Moya explained. 'That was another thing Greg invented. We unicorns have a stripe of coloured hair on the backs of our heads. Years ago, before all the portal openers were destroyed, unicorns sometimes travelled between the UNIverse and the human world and they had to hide their stripe of bright hair. But it was hard, especially if you had short hair. So Greg invented mullets. The long bit at the back hides the unicorn hair stripe perfectly. Then humans started cutting their hair like that. Mullets were very popular for a while, apparently.'

'You still haven't told me the story about Greg,' Neon pointed out. 'And the whole horse-with-a-horn thing.'

'Oh, that,' Moya said, as she pushed open the doors to Goohead Central.

Neon gasped. Through the grand front doors was a staircase made of luminous glass. Strands of neon lights snaked up the sides, next to floating globs of goo that glowed brightly. It was like standing in a giant packet of sweets that someone was shining a torch into.

To her left and right were corridors decorated in the same fashion as the stairs. People filed past, stopping and gasping and dropping things when they saw Neon.

'A long time ago,' Moya explained, as she took a left

and completely ignored the shocked faces around them, 'the word "unicorn" became known in the human world and spread. Humans began to hunt unicorns so they could find our world – more and more humans got involved as the years went on. It grew into a crisis. So the Gooheads asked everyone in the UNIverse to suggest ideas to fix the problem and keep our world safe and secret. That's where Greg comes in.'

'I still don't understand what that has to do with horses with horns,' Neon shouted after her, as she tried to keep up *and* dodge the lumps of floating goo.

'Greg's idea was to make up a horse-with-a-horn character and call it a unicorn. He said it would become so popular it would distract the humans, then *real* unicorns would remain a secret.'

The lights in the corridor seemed to pulse as they passed, faster and faster, as though they were getting closer to something. It was as if the building knew they were there.

'At first everyone thought it was a stupid idea,' Moya went on, throwing her hands in the air for dramatic effect. '"What a stupid idea, Greg!" they all said. But now Greg is laughing and he's a hero, because it worked. Apparently you can't go anywhere in the human world these days without seeing a unicorn backpack or a unicorn hairband or a unicorn cake, or even a unicorn *book*. The humans have gone unicorn mad!'

Neon nodded. 'That's true.'

'And our secret is safe!' Moya cheered.

Up ahead, just beyond the squiggles of sculpted light, Neon could make out a door.

'Here we go,' Moya said. 'I really hope they let you stay for a while!'

Inside, the room was bathed in a vivid yellow glow. And in the middle of the room, on a perfect crescent-moon table, sat four substantial jars of goo.

Inside the goo, four heads turned to face them.

'Meet the Gooheads,' Moya said proudly.

Neon screamed.

'I THOUGHT IT WAS A WEIRD FAMILY NAME!

YOU KNOW, MEET THE GOOHEADS … THEY'RE JUST HEADS IN GOO?!'

'Just heads in goo?' one of them said, sounding offended.

'I suppose she's technically correct,' another replied.

Neon screamed again. The Gooheads screamed back.

Four heads.

One green, one purple, one yellow, one blue.

In goo.

Screaming their heads ... well, not *off*, but, you know, they were SCREAMING.

'SO THIS IS THE HUMAN WHO UNCOVERED OUR SECRET?' the purple head screamed.

'OF *ALL* THE HUMANS IN THE WORLD!' the yellow one screamed.

'WHY ARE WE SCREAMING?' the green one screamed.

'BECAUSE THE GIRL IS!' the blue one screamed in reply. 'IT'S ONLY POLITE!'

Moya cleared her throat. 'If I may interrupt the hysteria, your Gooeynesses ... Neon is very nice. I think she'd be good at keeping our secret. Can she stay a while so I can show her around the UNIverse?'

The Gooheads stopped screaming and squelched in their jars, pressing their noses against the glass to get a better look at Neon.

'Welcome, human,' the green head said spookily.

'What are you?' Neon whispered.

'Pay attention! We're the Gooheads!' the purple head said. 'And we oversee the UNIverse. We're the ones who must decide what to do with you. Please let me see the portal opener.'

Neon stepped forward and placed the lipstick on the table.

As quick as a flash, one of several bright wires dropped from the ceiling, wrapped itself around the lipstick and lifted it away.

'No!' Neon cried. 'I NEED THAT TO GET HOME!'

The Gooheads shook their heads.

'I'm afraid that lipstick belongs to us,' the purple head said.

'I won't tell anyone about any of this,' Neon said nervously. 'I actually wouldn't want to! If you'll let me explain. I'm on a quest to be norm—'

'No time!' the purple head interrupted. 'We're very busy today. I'm afraid it's the goo pits for you.'

'NO!' Moya cried, making Neon jump.

'What are the goo pits?' Neon asked.

'They are the *pits*,' Moya said with a shudder. 'Once

you go in, you never come out. You live your life in a terrible goo and see terrible things, it's just—'

'Terrible?' Neon guessed.

'Problem is, she hasn't done anything wrong,' the blue head pointed out. 'The goo pits are for criminals, and people who annoy us. It wouldn't be right to put her there. Not yet anyway.'

The purple head rolled its eyes. 'We can't release a human back into the human world and just *hope* they won't tell our secret. The humans can never know – imagine what the last remaining Unicorn Hunters would do if they could prove unicorns aren't horses with horns!'

'So what do you suggest?' the green head asked.

'She stays here forever and lives with the McGlows,' the purple head said. 'Problem solved.'

Moya gasped. 'A SISTER! Oh I LOVE that idea!'

'But I already have a family!' Neon cried. 'And a life in the human world. I can't just disappear. They'd worry!'

'She's right,' the yellow head said. 'She's can't stay here when she has a life *there*.'

'Hmm … what *if*,' the purple head said, 'there was a chance it might not be forever? What if Neon became a magical unicorn?'

'YES!' Moya roared, punching the air with delight.

'Not with hooves and a mane, *please*,' Neon said.

The purple Goohead rolled its eyes. 'Not a Greg unicorn, Neon. A real one, like Moya. To become one of us, you need to learn to command goo. If you succeed, a streak of colour grows into your hair and you get your official papers. Oh, and it has to be done before you reach the age of ten. How old are you, Neon?'

'My tenth birthday is in a few days,' Neon said quietly.

'Ooh,' the yellow head said to the purple head. 'I see where you're going with this.'

'Well, that's perfect – you have until midnight on your tenth birthday to learn to command goo and become a magical unicorn,' the purple Goohead announced grandly. 'If you succeed, *then* we'll let you go home.'

'Why then?' Neon pressed.

'Because,' the purple Goohead explained, 'if you're a magical unicorn, then our secret becomes *your* secret too. You'd never tell the humans, because if you did, *you* would be in as much danger as us.'

'Ah!' Moya said, clapping. 'Clever!'

'What exactly does "command goo" mean?' Neon asked.

'You must be able to use magic goos correctly, without accident or incident,' the purple Goohead explained. 'Most goos come with instructions, some do not. Many require stretching, splatting, or exact measurements. Others you'll need to tip on to your head …'

Neon nodded, taking it all in. Commanding goo didn't sound too difficult.

'Did it take you long to command goo?' she asked Moya.

'Ages!' Moya replied. 'Most unicorns start from birth and learn for ten years. The world of goo can be bewildering at first!'

'Ten years?! I don't even have ten days!' Neon cried. 'Who decides if I can command goo or not?'

'The UNIverse,' the purple Goohead said mysteriously. 'Only it can decide if you are worthy of goo.'

'And what happens if it decides someone is not worthy?' Neon asked.

'Then after their tenth birthday magic goo won't work for them ever again,' the purple Goohead said. 'No colourful streak of hair or magical abilities. Of course, you'll have the added sting of being stuck here forever.'

'But don't worry,' Moya said quickly. 'You'll do it! Almost everyone does.'

'Greg didn't,' the green Goohead said.

'Wait, *the* Greg failed?' Neon said in disbelief. 'The UNIverse didn't think he was worthy of goo? He has no magical abilities?'

The Gooheads shook their gooey heads.

'Greg was dreadful with goo,' the purple Goohead said. 'We were all very relieved when he turned ten and it stopped working for him. He's just a corn now.'

'A corn?' Neon said with a raised eyebrow.

'A non-magical unicorn,' the Gooheads said in unison. 'A corn.'

'So, do we have a deal?' the purple Goohead asked.

Neon crossed her arms and considered her options. She could stay trapped in the UNIverse forever, or try to become a magical unicorn so the Gooheads would let her go home …

'Fine,' Neon said. 'I'll try to become a magical unicorn. But there's a problem – my parents still won't know where I am and they'll be so worried, even if I'm only gone for a day.'

The Gooheads exchanged amused glances.

'Decoy time!' the yellow head said.

And with a *bang*, a perfect replica of Neon appeared in front of her.

'Woah!' Neon cried. 'It's me!'

'I like rats,' decoy Neon chirped.

Neon prodded the decoy.

'I like rats,' it said again.

'We'll send the decoy to the human world in your place. She's a temporary goo and will disappear when she meets you again. Unfortunately, for legal reasons, we could only give her one phrase.'

'I like rats!' the decoy said.

'Please,' Neon begged, 'can the phrase be *anything* other than that? I'm really trying to be normal in the human world.'

The decoy disappeared with a *pop*.

'Sorry,' the purple Goohead said. 'The phrase has already been set.'

'The decoy can say it in a happy way or a sad way or any sort of way, really, so no one will suspect a thing!' the yellow Goohead cheered.

Neon shook her head in silent annoyance.

'There's another problem,' Moya said, taking a step forward. 'Neon hasn't been at school in the UNIverse, and it's the school holidays … goo can be expensive and she has no UNIverse money. How will she get goo to practise her commanding?'

The Gooheads smiled.

'Well,' the purple Goohead said, 'I suppose Neon will have to find a job.'

'Find a job?' Neon said. 'I'm NINE.'

'Pah!' the purple Goohead said. 'That's no excuse!'

7

The Goomart

Back in the centre of Lumino, Neon was – much to her surprise – in search of a job.

'What about the Goomart?' Neon said, pushing through the crowds.

She pressed her palms against one of the windows. It was piled high with pots of goo in every colour – some had sparkles in them, others had little jelly stars or chunks of rainbow. Some were lurid green, others luminous pink. In fact, there was every colour you could imagine, with every kind of sparkle you could imagine too. A sign read:

THE UNIverse'S NO. 1 GENUINE EVERY
KIND OF GOO SHOP
FOR ALL YOUR MAGIC NEEDS!

There were goos for everything, if the labels were to be believed. Cauldron of Candy goo, Haunted House goo, Angry Monster goo, Skeleton Ballet goo (it was coming up for Halloween, so they had a monster theme in the window). Big Hair goo, Short Hair goo, Cupid goo ...

Peeling posters in glittering print cluttered the windows, advertising sweet goos for birthday parties and decoration goos for something called Scarlett Night. And right in the middle was a large advert:

WANTED: GOOMART CASHIER!
Passionate about goo? Know your discount Witch goo from your Glitter Slide goo? Then come and work for us!
From assisting unicorns with their daily shop to sourcing the perfect goo for a special customer, the job is NEVER boring.
(WARNING: Will involve cleaning up goo spillages, which could result in: drastic changes to your facial hair, growing new feet, attacks by

monsters, witches and vampires, glitter hallucin-
ations, entrapment in temporary and often
terrifying magical worlds, death, and other
much, much worse things.)
To apply, join the try-outs in-store at 11 a.m. this
Thursday!
Please bring a helmet.

Neon looked at the town clock. It was 10.58.

'You're just in time!' Moya cheered.

'Looking for a goo?' came a voice, making them both jump.

Neon turned to see an old woman in a sparkling silver dress with ruffled sleeves and a gooey-looking belt. She wore goo-drip earrings and her hair was white with a streak of purple through it.

'Old Lady Buck,' she said, extending a hand. 'I own this joint. And you must be the human everyone is talking about.'

Neon looked sheepishly at her shoes.

'Oh, word spreads quicker than mouldy goo in this

town,' Old Lady Buck said with a chuckle. 'Now, what can I get you?'

'I'm actually looking for a job,' Neon said.

'Well, come on in for the try-outs!' Old Lady Buck said, pointing at the job advert in the window. 'Everyone is welcome in the Goomart.'

Neon smiled. 'I love your shop – do you only sell goo?'

'Oh yes, most things in the UNIverse are goo until you command them. Every shop in town is filled with pots of goo. Mine is the best – it's the oldest shop in the UNIverse! Though if I had to pick another favourite shop, it would be the Slimy Wardrobe. Best clothes in town!' She pointed past Neon. 'Take a look!'

The Slimy Wardrobe was a luminous yellow shop with a glittering gold door.

Its windows were stuffed with goo pots wrapped in different fabrics. A shoe shop called Goo Heels stood next door, and across the road a pet shop called Whiskers & Gloop had a furry door and a slimy door handle. Beside it was Squelchie's Story Shop, filled to the brim with book-sized slices of goo.

Neon smiled. 'It's all very … gooey.'

The town clock jingled and sprayed glitter across the busy square, coating nearby unicorns from head to toe. It was eleven o'clock.

Neon looked at Old Lady Buck. 'Let's do this,' she said with a big grin.

Old Lady Buck pushed open the glittering double doors. 'Welcome, Neon, to the GOOMART!'

Neon couldn't believe her eyes.

Inside, shoppers with horseshoe-shaped shopping baskets trotted up and down goo-pot-filled aisles. The place was huge and humming with magic.

Everyone ground to a halt when they saw Neon.

'Yes, yes,' Moya said, marching in, her shoes clopping on the sparkling floor. 'Neon's a human and it's not a big deal! She's staying for a while, so let's not gawp. She might be working here soon!'

Neon waved shyly. Everyone got back to their shopping.

'Small thing,' Old Lady Buck whispered. 'Being a

human who mistakenly sort of fell into our world, you didn't happen to bring a helmet with you, did you?'

'No,' Neon said. 'Oh, it says bring a helmet on the job advert. Can I do the try-outs without one?'

'Of course,' Old Lady Buck said. 'You're not hugely attached to your head, are you?'

Neon couldn't quite understand why anyone would need a helmet to help unicorns find jars of goo and run them through the checkout tills.

A tinkling noise sounded and Old Lady Buck's voice crackled over the tannoy.

'Good Uni-day, shoppers! We'll now be holding try-outs for our new GOOMART CASHIER. And for safety purposes the store will be closing for one hour. Please proceed to the checkout and complete your purchases.'

As the shoppers busied themselves adding the last pots of goo to their baskets, Neon took the opportunity to check out her competition.

There were three others in total. One girl had glowing red hair with a slash of yellow running through the back of it. She wore a sequined dress with a high neck and matching cape, paired with rainbow-striped tights and jelly shoes just like Neon's. Her face was pinched into a sour expression and she had her eyes fixed on the aisles, ready to go.

Next to her was a shy-looking boy, biting nervously at his nails. He was wearing purple dungarees with a blue knitted jumper covered in glitter stars. He had a thin streak of blue through the back of his curly hair.

'Why do some unicorns have a thicker coloured streak than others?' Neon asked.

'The bigger the streak, the better command of goo the unicorn has,' Moya explained.

Neon stared at the girl with the red hair and gulped. Her yellow streak was at least six inches wide. 'She must be good …' Neon mumbled.

The third contestant was a boy so tall and lanky he towered over everyone in the shop. He was wearing a racing-green tracksuit and had already put his helmet on. And it wasn't just any old helmet. It had a protective visor and grille covering his face, and about six layers of padding.

Neon watched in horror as the other two pulled out their helmets.

'I'm scared,' she blurted out to Moya. 'The helmets look really serious.'

'You know,' Moya said, 'there's a famous song we sing to baby unicorns when they feel afraid. Even now it never fails to make me feel better. Listen!

'Don't be afraid, little unicorn,
because the clouds in the sky are still there!
Don't be afraid, little unicorn,
because the glitter in the world is still here!'

Neon found herself bobbing along to the song. It did make her feel better!

'Don't be afraid, little unicorn,
because the UNIverse is still filled with glee!

And don't be afraid, little unicorn,
because you could be one of those rubbish
humans, and they can't even comm-a-and goo!'

Moya finished and beamed at Neon. 'See? Always makes me feel better.'

'But I *am* a human,' Neon said flatly.

'Oh,' Moya winced. 'Right ...'

'Now,' Old Lady Buck said, 'who do we have here? Filly Spangle!'

The girl in the sequined dress stepped forward and smirked.

'Bronco Blazon!'

The nervous boy raised his hand.

'And Geldie O'Splendid!'

The tall boy did two thumbs up.

'After Greg made up the horse-with-a-horn thing,' Moya whispered to Neon, 'it became really fashionable to give baby unicorns horsey names ...'

'And finally,' Old Lady Buck said with a cough to get their attention, 'our new favourite human, Neon Gallup!'

The other contestants turned and stared at her.

'Hellooooo,' Neon found herself saying in a silly voice. *Ugh*, she thought. *Be normal.*

'And are you here to apply for the job?' Old Lady Buck asked Moya.

'No, I'm here to watch Neon win!' Moya cheered.

Old Lady Buck cracked a smile. 'All right, but please watch from outside the window, for safety reasons.'

Moya nodded obediently and raced out of the door.

'Your first test is a simple customer shopping list,' Old Lady Buck said as she handed out lists on twinkling paper to each of the contestants. 'Each item can be found on its own, but I want you to find the *one* goo that will provide the customer with all three of these things in one pot.'

Neon stared at the list.

MAGIC UNICORN TEAPOT GOO
DANCING AND SINGING CAKE GOO
SUNSHINE PICNIC GOO

'You have one minute!' Old Lady Buck bellowed. And with a click of her stopwatch, the contestants were off.

Neon ran aimlessly down the aisles, occasionally catching a glimpse of the goo jar labels.

HAIRSPRAY GOO … CHEESE GOO … SWIMMING POOL OF DOOM GOO …

She looked above the aisles to the section categories and spotted *CAKES*. She tore towards it, colliding with Geldie as she went.

'Ten seconds!' Old Lady Buck called.

As much as Neon's heart was thumping in her mouth with worry, she was relieved the helmets seemed unnecessary. In fact, her main worry was that only she and Geldie were in the cake aisle. She was even more worried when she realised his helmet had so much padding he couldn't really see out of it.

'TIME'S UP!' Old Lady Buck yelled. 'Please bring your jars of goo to the checkout.'

Neon grabbed a goo pot from the shelf and raced back to the others. She hadn't even had time to read the label.

'Hmm,' Old Lady Buck said, inspecting each jar. 'Neon has got the right idea by going with a cake goo. She has chosen a VERY FUNNY CAKE GOO.'

Neon beamed. Had she done it?!

'Unfortunately,' Old Lady Buck said, 'this goo doesn't provide tea or sunshine. The customer would be very disappointed indeed, though they would probably enjoy the cake's jokes. Still, wrong goo, I'm afraid!'

'Oh,' Neon said sadly, feeling like she might cry. The sight of Moya outside the shop, waving a hastily made *GO, NEON!* sign, made her feel better.

Second through the checkout was Bronco. He had chosen a completely incorrect HAM SANDWICH GOO.

'I panicked!' he squealed.

'Ah, now we have something!' Old Lady Buck said. 'Both Filly and Geldie have correctly picked up the GREGILICIOUS 3-IN-1 PICNIC GOO. And that is exactly what the customer needed.'

'If you'd already picked up the correct goo,' Neon whispered to Geldie, 'then why were you in the cake aisle?'

He lifted the visor on his helmet. 'I was trying to help you,' he whispered. 'I was telling you what you needed, but I don't think you heard me through all the padding.'

'Oh,' Neon said. 'Thanks.'

Geldie had a kind smile and Neon thought he looked familiar, but there was no way she could have met him before.

'No problem,' he said with a nod, making the visor snap back down.

'What does the 3-IN-1 PICNIC GOO do?' Neon asked. She was itching to see some magic.

'You don't know?' Filly said, sounding irritated. 'Why are you applying for a job at the Goomart if you don't know?'

'We'll try it out,' Old Lady Buck said, unscrewing the jar. She pulled out some goo, which she rolled and stretched between her fingers. There was a *BANG* and suddenly the shop was bathed in blazing sunshine. Picnic rugs unfurled under their feet and pretty, glowing vines climbed the shelves around them. She swung the goo around her head, and with a *FLASH* a giant cake fell with a splat into Neon's arms and began singing and jiggling. For the finale, Old Lady Buck rolled the goo into a tight ball and threw it on the floor. With a *SNAP*, a teapot appeared in a puff of smoke and started spurting tea and unicorns. The horse kind – the Greg kind. They galloped around, neighing madly and swishing their rainbow tails.

'Incredible,' Neon whispered.

'Watch your face!' Old Lady Buck cried as a unicorn charged past Neon, leaving a trail of glitter in its wake.

Filly grabbed a fistful of cake, which made the cake's singing voice quieter. 'When's the next challenge?' she said, sounding impatient.

Old Lady Buck pressed the button on the tannoy. 'CLEAN-UP AT THE CHECKOUT!'

The cake in Neon's arms seemed to sing louder and almost wriggled from her grasp.

'CLEAN-UP AT THE CHECKOUT!' Old Lady Buck cried again.

This time, a young boy came pelting out of the back room wearing gloves and waving a gooey wand. He tore down the vines and used them as a lasso to catch the unicorns, then he touched them with the wand and they disappeared with a *pop*, spraying glitter all over the shop and into Neon's gawping mouth.

'This is my nephew Buckee,' Old Lady Buck explained. 'He's helping me until I find someone to fill the position.'

Neon spluttered and coughed up a ball of glitter. 'Please let it be me,' she wheezed.

The next task was a checkout challenge, which involved scanning as many jars of goo as possible in one minute without breaking any of them. Neon didn't break a single jar, and for a moment she felt like a proper, fully-fledged unicorn. But no one else broke any jars either, so they all passed that one.

'Unusual not to have at least one spillage,' Old Lady Buck said. 'Well done to you all. Ordinarily, I use the spillage as the clean-up task in the next challenge, but since we have no spillages, I'll just have to spill one of my own …'

8

The Goomart, Part Two

Old Lady Buck handed them each a goo wand. Neon's was orange with tiny stars inside it.

'Cool,' she said, holding it aloft.

'To clean up a goo, Neon, you need to hold the wand against it for a few seconds,' Old Lady Buck explained, then she grabbed a jar at random and smashed it on the floor. 'Good luck, everyone.'

'What was it?' Bronco asked, his eyes wide with terror.

A putrid orange smoke wafted around them.

'No idea,' Old Lady Buck said with a giggle. 'But judging by the orange smoke, I'd say it's one of the Halloween special goos.'

'The whole thing?' Bronco said nervously. 'The whole thing is out of the jar?!'

Neon shivered. The air around them had grown colder and she could see her breath clouding in front of her.

'This looks like a SCARY ONE!' Old Lady Buck shouted. 'Helmets on!'

Outside the window, Moya was looking worried.

Neon turned back just in time to see a strange creature emerging from the smoke. He was tall, with huge fangs and a lace ruff around his neck.

'VAMPIIIIIIIIRE!' Bronco screeched, before tearing off down one of the aisles.

'Oh no, *not* the novelty vampires,' Filly groaned. 'They're *so* boring.'

The vampire's eyes flashed orange and he cracked his neck from left to right. Slowly, he reached his long spindly fingers into his cape and pulled out –

'ROLLER SKATES?!' Neon cried, as Geldie grabbed her arm and began to run.

'IT'S EVEN WORSE THAN A VAMPIRE! IT'S A ROLLER-SKATING VAMPIRE!' Bronco roared, zigzagging up and down the aisle ahead of them and smacking head first into a wall. 'I surrender,' he whimpered.

Neon ran to help him.

'Good job you were wearing a helmet!' she said, looking up to see the vampire skating fast in their direction. He snapped his jaws.

'COME ON!' Neon cried, pulling the boy to safety. They ran until they found Geldie.

'Where's Filly?' Neon asked.

Everything had gone strangely silent. Neon listened carefully, but she couldn't hear the snapping of the vampire's jaws, or even the sinister scraping of roller skates.

Hastily, she climbed the shelves to get a view of the entire shop.

Filly was in aisle twelve, holding her goo wand and creeping forward slowly.

Neon gasped – the vampire was sneaking up behind her.

'BEHIND YOU, FILLY!' Neon cried.

But it was too late. The vampire shot forward and scooped Filly into his arms!

'NO! NOT FILLY!' Neon roared as she watched the vampire skate off ... to the checkout, where Filly was scanned and dropped into a shopping bag.

'Hang on a minute,' Neon said.

Filly then started flashing like a disco light, glowing red, green, yellow, orange, purple and pink from her hair to her shoes.

'All that happens is you start flashing like a light?' Neon cried. 'I thought we were going to be KILLED.'

'THAT LIGHT EFFECT CAN LAST FOR HOURS! I CAN'T DO THIS!' Bronco roared, and he tore off down the aisle and straight out of the shop.

The roller-skating vampire turned his head and snarled at Neon.

'He saw me!' Neon shouted.

She tried to climb down, but her foot got caught and she slipped, pulling the shelves down with her! Jars smashed everywhere and goo squelched under her shoes as she clumsily backed away from the mess.

'AAARGH, WHAT HAVE YOU DONE?!' Geldie

shouted. Neon could hear him this time, even through the padding.

She stared up nervously at the section of the Goomart they were in:

HALLOWEEN DELIGHTS!

'*Now* we have a clean-up challenge!' Old Lady Buck cheered through the tannoy.

Neon fell to her hands and knees and desperately tried to scoop the goo back into the broken jars. Frogs were bouncing out of one and another was chanting, '*Dun dun duuuun.*' Smoke filled the air, along with the sound of cackles.

Geldie raised the visor on his helmet. 'Halloween is coming, Neon. *All of it.*'

'Maybe it won't be so bad,' she said hopefully. She plucked a label from the mess: *SUPER CUTE AND CUDDLY WITCHES*.

'That doesn't sound bad at all!' Neon said, as ten cute, tiny ghost witches no bigger than sparrows began aggressively hugging her face.

'MET MOFF MEE!' Neon cried, but one of the ghost witches grabbed her tongue and began using it as a skipping rope.

The goo on the floor began to bubble! Spindly fingers crept out of the slime! Skeletons rose up and began doing ballet! Brooms shot into the air and cauldrons and pumpkins rolled around the aisles! Zombies clawed their way across the floor and more roller-skating vampires put on their skates!

'We can't clean these up with our goo wands – it'll take FOREVER,' Geldie fretted. 'We've lost.'

'Isn't there a goo that will undo them?' Neon asked.

Geldie shook his head. 'There's no single goo that can undo all of Halloween!'

Neon stood frozen to the spot, an idea forming. 'I THINK THERE IS A GOO THAT CAN UNDO ALL OF HALLOWEEN!' she cried, shaking the little ghost witches from her face and propelling herself on to a flying broom. 'COME ON, GELDIE!'

'HOW CAN YOU KNOW A GOO?' he said as he

threw himself on to a neighbouring broom. 'YOU ONLY FOUND OUT GOO *EXISTS* ABOUT AN HOUR AGO!'

They shot off across the shop.

'AHA!' Neon said, spying the *OUT OF SEASON* section.

'How is that a good idea?' Geldie called after her.

Neon dismounted the broom and gestured at a very specific shelf.

'Christmas?' Geldie said, falling down next to her.

'What gets rid of Halloween things in the shops every year?' Neon asked.

Geldie looked blank.

'It's Christmas things! Haven't you noticed how the *second* Halloween is over the shops are filled with Christmas things?'

She grabbed a pot of BIG OLD JOLLY SANTA GOO and smashed it on the floor.

'You know, you can just open the jars you want to use,' Geldie said. 'Also, I think that Santa one requires precise measurement, otherwise—'

A figure was emerging from the puddle of red goo

on the floor. It grew bigger and bigger until its head hit the ceiling.

'SANTA!' Neon cheered.

'And what would you like for Chris—?' Santa began, but he stopped when he saw the mess in the Halloween section.

'IT'S *MY* SEASON NOW!' he bellowed, before bouncing off. 'MIIIIIIIIIINE!'

Neon watched, amazed, as he scooped up the roller-skating vampires and the zombies and the tiny ghost witches, and *all* the fingers, plucked the gravestones from the floor and disassembled the coffins, collected the cauldrons and rounded up the pumpkins.

'I think I did it,' Neon said in disbelief.

Geldie rushed over and pressed the goo wand against Santa.

With a *pop* and a puff of festive glitter, he vanished.

'NEON, THAT WAS AMAZING!' came Moya's muffled shout from the other side of the window.

'Very good,' Old Lady Buck said, clapping her way towards them. 'A neat little solution to a very messy problem.' She looked Neon up and down. 'Especially impressive given you've been a human your whole life.'

Moya came bursting through the doors. 'Is Neon getting the job? Has she got the job?'

'Please wait outside,' Old Lady Buck ordered Moya.

Moya raced back to her spot by the window and stood there with her fingers crossed and her eyes squeezed shut.

'Decisions, decisions,' Old Lady Buck said. 'Geldie did very well on the first two tasks, but without Neon on the last task, things wouldn't have been so neatly tidied up.' She stood tapping her foot for a moment.

Neon wished with all her might that she'd get it. She *needed* the job, she needed it more than anyone else!

'I've decided you can *both* have a job,' Old Lady Buck finally said. 'Geldie, you'll work the checkouts and assist customers with special shopping requests. Neon, you'll take on the newly created role of Goo Spillage Human.'

Neon felt so happy she thought she might explode.

Old Lady Buck handed them some golds – unicorn money, stamped with Greg's face – and told them to visit the Slimy Wardrobe to buy their uniforms. 'And you can keep the goo wands.'

Neon looked around the Goomart and beamed. 'Thank you, Old Lady Buck, I won't let you down!'

'You'll be paid at the end of every working day, Neon, so you can afford one jar of goo a day to practise with. Now, you'd better go and tell your friend the news,' Old Lady Buck said, gesturing to Moya, who had smooshed her whole face against the glass.

'I will! See you tomorrow,' Neon said to Old Lady Buck and Geldie, as she made her way towards the door. She felt like she was floating, she couldn't believe it, she just couldn't believe that she'd got the –

A gigantic ghostly rat stopped her dead in her tracks. He was twice her height and wore a three-piece suit.

'Greetings and welcome to aisle five,' he said. 'I hear congratulations are in order.'

Neon looked around for Old Lady Buck and Geldie, but they'd gone.

'Um, are you a Halloween goo?' she asked the ghost rat.

'*Please*,' the rat said with a flourish of his paw. 'I'm much more special than *that*. I'm  over a hundred years old and I was made from the finest goo, back when this place sold the proper stuff, not the novelty, mass-produced goos they sell now. They've tried to clean me up for decades, but they can't!'

'Why not?' Neon asked.

'Can't catch me,' the rat said proudly 'Fast-moving, often invisible. Made from the same goo the Gooheads themselves live in. No one ever has or ever will be able to clean me up.' He eyed the goo wand in Neon's hand. 'And I'd suggest you never try, new Goo Spillage Human.'

'I won't,' Neon said with a gulp. She wasn't going to mess with a giant ghost rat. If he'd lived there for over a hundred years, he could live there for a hundred years more as far as she was concerned.

'I look forward to seeing you around then, Neon Gallup,' the rat said, before floating through the shelves and vanishing from sight.

'DID YOU GET IT?' Moya asked, springing from foot to foot in the doorway. 'DID YOU GET IT?'

Neon proudly held up the golds.

9

The Slimy Wardrobe

'Um, Moya … strange question for you,' Neon said as they walked into the Slimy Wardrobe. 'Have you ever heard of a giant ghost rat who lives in the Goomart?'

Moya nodded. 'That's Alaric. He likes to scare the customers. They've been trying to clean him up for years – most unicorns are TERRIFIED of him, but I don't mind him, to be honest. He gives good shopping tips. Now – uniform section …'

The Slimy Wardrobe was very narrow, but much taller than it looked from the outside. Neon could see a rickety green staircase that went up and up past what must have been at least ten floors of gowns and goo pots.

They made their way to the back of the first floor,

where dozens of different uniforms hung on mannequins with fake goo hair.

'That's the one you need,' Moya said, pointing at a sparkling purple apron with *Goomart* on it and a matching pair of padded gloves.

A helpful assistant plucked a jar of goo from the display and handed it to Neon.

GOOMART OFFICIAL UNIFORM
Please see bottom of tub for sizing instructions.

'My first proper attempt at commanding goo!' Neon cried.

Unfortunately, Neon didn't read the small print, and in her excitement pulled the whole glob of goo out. It began to spit glitter before morphing into an apron and gloves about ten sizes too big for her.

'How do you make them smaller?' Neon asked innocently.

The sales assistant tutted. 'You take the right amount of goo out of the pot in the first place, that's how.'

'Sorry,' Moya mouthed to her. 'Hu-man.'

The sales assistant held out her hand for the golds.

'Can I try again?' Neon asked.

'No,' the sales assistant said, taking the golds and disappearing up the stairs.

'It's all right,' Moya said. 'We can tie bits of it together and make it fit you. And then, when you get paid tomorrow, we can always buy some shrink goo.'

'You mean I have to wear this?' Neon said, pulling the apron over her head. It drowned her like an over-sized ball gown. She put on a glove – it was massive.

Moya checked her watch. 'It's getting late, we'd better get home. My parents might want us to help with the Scarlett Night decorations.'

'Scarlett Night?' Neon said. 'I saw a poster about it in the Goomart window. What is it?'

'Only the scariest night in the UNIverse,' Moya said. 'It's tomorrow, but my parents like to make sure the decorations are really good – she's less likely to haunt you if you've got good decorations.'

Neon shivered. '*Who* is less likely to haunt you?'

'Scarlett,' Moya said gravely. 'She's the worst goo ever to escape into the UNIverse, and soon she'll be here …'

10

Moya's House

Moya lived a few streets from the Goomart, in a bright row of houses painted in every colour of the rainbow. Hers was pink. The door was decorated with a Greg unicorn, Greg-unicorn curtains hung at the windows and models of Greg unicorns galloped across the roof.

'The neighbours hate it,' Moya said as she and Neon strolled up the street. 'But we're Greg SUPERFANS and we're LOUD about it.'

Many of the neighbours were outside their houses, stringing up bright red lanterns displaying the same sinister face. One was hanging a gooey wreath on her door and waved at Moya as they passed.

'Scarlett Night decorations,' Moya explained, climbing the steps to her house.

Neon could see a sign on the door that read: *UNICORN CUPBOARD*.

'I named the house that,' Moya said proudly, throwing open the door. 'I love cupboards.'

'And unicorns,' Neon said flatly, taking in what lay inside. 'Greg-style.'

The wallpaper was unicorn patterned, the carpet was unicorn patterned. Anything that wasn't unicorn patterned was unicorn shaped – like the big mirror hanging in the hallway, which took the form of a big unicorn head. Neon stopped dead in her tracks as she passed it.

'W-w-wait … W-w-why am I—?' she stared at herself in the mirror, grabbing her cheeks and pulling at them. Her reflection was showing Neon as a unicorn! The Greg kind, the *horse* kind.

'Great, isn't it?' Moya said. 'All you need is simple Greg Unicorn Transformation goo to spread on the mirror and it turns your reflection into the Greg unicorn version of you. You have a fabulous mane!'

Neon stroked her hair and, in the mirror, a hoof appeared and stroked a bouffant sparkly green mane.

She looked down at her hands to check they hadn't transformed into hooves. Anything seemed possible in the UNIverse …

'Moya!' came a cry, as two adults clad head to toe in crazy unicorn-patterned clothes came trotting down the hallway. 'And Neon! The Gooheads have briefed us. You're so welcome here! Wonderful to have you.'

'Thank you, Mr and Mrs McGlow,' Neon said.

'We've made dinner – you must be starving after nearly ten years in the human world. I've heard the food there is terrible!' Moya's dad said.

'And we had some spare Greg goo to make an extra bed for you in Moya's bedroom,' Moya's mum said. 'Why don't you go and get yourself settled and have a glitter shower before we eat?'

'Come on,' Moya cried, grabbing Neon and taking the stairs two at a time.

Moya's room was – as expected – covered in unicorn-patterned stuff. And her bed was shaped like the front half of a unicorn. Neon's was, unexpectedly, the … rear end.

She thought back to the moment she'd found the lipstick – had she known then that it would lead to her falling into a different world, being told by some heads in goo that she wasn't allowed to leave and then having to sleep in a bed shaped like a unicorn's bottom, she probably would have quietly put it back.

'Do you want to see my shoe collection?' Moya said excitedly. 'I've been making and collecting Greg-unicorn shoes my whole life!'

She threw open her wardrobe to reveal a walk-in room filled with hundreds of shelves of shoes.

Some had manes, like her trainers. Others had horns. Neon picked up a pair of big platform shoes shaped like hooves.

'Oh, those are Moya's favourite,' her dad said as he appeared behind them. 'But they're almost impossible to walk in.'

'I'm only allowed to wear them if I use my unicorn crutches,' Moya explained cheerily, producing a pair of appropriately patterned crutches.

Neon laughed. Maybe staying in the UNIverse until her tenth birthday might not be so bad after all.

Every mirror in the McGlow household was covered in the Greg Unicorn Transformation goo, and every time Neon walked past one, she leaped in fright.

Dinner was spaghetti, and each strand was a different colour. It was followed by Neigh Whip Unicorn Cones that looked a lot like ice cream cones, only the 'ice cream' was a fluffy substance that made you neigh when you ate it.

'We'd better put the Scarlett Night decorations up after supper,' Mr McGlow said, as the others finished the last of their cones.

'*Neeeeigh!*' replied Moya.

'Is Scarlett Night like Halloween?' Neon asked. '*NEIGH.*'

'Not really,' Moya said. 'Halloween can be fun, but Scarlett Night is just plain scary. Scarlett, the escaped Villain Goo returns in search of something, but no one knows quite what it is.'

'Where did she come from?' Neon asked.

'A long time ago, she was made as a villain goo for a book – you know, a wicked witch, a jewel thief, an evil overlord. That kind of thing. She could have been anything – she has various evil laughs and voices and is a big ball of different types of villain. Writers used to buy character goos to inspire their stories, but ever since Scarlett escaped, they don't sell them any more.'

'How did she escape?' Neon asked.

'Well, Greg was the one who bought the goo,' Moya said. 'When he was five.'

'Oh no,' Neon whispered.

'He wanted to write a story about baddies,' Moya went on. 'He tried to use the villian goo, but he didn't read the instructions properly. Scarlett took off, and the rest is history!'

'I can see why Greg is a corn,' Neon said.

'Scarlett returns every year, on the anniversary of her escape. Usually she just makes a mess of the decorations we put up for her,' Mrs McGlow said. '*Neigh!*'

'That's why everyone puts up decorations,' Moya went on. 'Because a long time ago we realised that she'll spend hours angrily destroying them. They work as a decoy, to stop her spoiling things we actually care about. It gives her something to focus on. She seems almost lost, really – a villain floating around the UNIverse without a purpose.'

'Has anyone tried to clean her up?' Neon asked.

'Oh yes,' Mr McGlow said gravely. 'But none of those unicorns lived to tell the tale. After a while, we gave up trying and decided to put up with her – one night of the year isn't too bad.'

'We stay inside, armed with goo, and watch as she rages through the UNIverse,' Moya said. 'The sky burns red, everything feels

sinister, and then the next day we clean up, and it's over!'

'Can't wait,' Neon mumbled. She didn't like the sound of Scarlett Night *at all*.

That night, Neon and Moya stayed up late chatting.

'What if I can't command goo before my birthday?' Neon asked quietly. 'What if I don't become a magical unicorn, Moya?'

'You will,' Moya said confidently. 'You're Neon Gallup, and even though I've only known you since this morning, I really feel it in my unicorn platform-hoof shoes, that you can do anything! Just look at what you did with that Christmas goo.'

'Thanks, Moya,' Neon said sleepily. 'I hope you're right.'

As they pulled their unicorn-patterned blankets up to their chins and closed their eyes, Moya whispered, 'Neon?'

'Yes?'

'I'm so happy you found the UNIverse.'

11

Feed Me Brains!

Two days until Neon's tenth birthday

Neon threw open the doors to the Goomart, ready to start her first day. She had intended to march in with purpose, but instead – because her apron was still ten times too big – she shuffled in slowly and fell flat on her face.

When she looked up, gentle pastel pink light was streaming through the windows, casting a magical glow across the place. Red Scarlett Night goo hung from the rafters and all around her unicorns were busy plucking pots of goo from the shelves. The checkouts *tinged* and Old Lady Buck's cheerful announcements rang out over the tannoy.

'Today is YELLOW GOO DAY, which means half

price on all yellow goos! Specials include the GIANT CHEESE goo and the RUBBER DUCK OF DESTRUCTION novelty goo. Oh, no – apologies. I have just been informed by our new cashier, Geldie O'Splendid, that we have sold out of RUBBER DUCK OF DESTRUCTION novelty goo. It's probably not a bad thing, assuming you don't want a giant duck to smash up your bathroom.'

The morning was non-stop clean-ups. The worst was when Neon slid face first into a particularly stinky purple goo spillage at the checkouts.

'Why does it smell like toilets?' she asked.

'Um …' Geldie said. 'Because it's MR UNI-BRUSH'S TOILET CLEANER GOO.'

'But toilet cleaner should smell clean,' Neon said, just as a large and very dirty toilet brush popped up from the goo and started aggressively brushing her hair.

'It's a really popular goo and has cleaned a lot of toilets already today,' Geldie explained.

'UGH, GROSS, YUCK!' Neon cried, trying to bat it away. 'I'M NOT A TOILET!!'

'It's her first day,' Geldie said apologetically to some horrified customers watching nearby. He lowered his voice to a whisper. 'She's also a *human*.'

The clean-ups were never-ending. It was usually something to do with Alaric, who liked to scare customers into dropping the jars they were holding. But Neon secretly loved his antics.

She didn't have any time to stand still – she was constantly batting things with her jumbo gloves and chasing things down the aisles with her goo wand. Cleaning up goo was teaching her so much about how different goos worked, but the more she learned, the more she realised she was going to need a lot of practice if she was going to command it correctly. The only commanding of goo she'd done was in the Slimy Wardrobe with the apron and gloves, and that had gone horribly wrong. And to add to her worries …

'WE DIDN'T MEAN IT!' two very young twin unicorns cried.

They handed Neon an open jar, along with the tiniest glob of goo.

'You opened the jar before buying it?' Neon said. 'Well, let's see what we're dealing with.' She inspected the label.

CREATE A GIANT HAIRY MONSTER, WITH FEARSOME CLAWS AND FEET SO BIG HE CAN RUN AROUND THE UNIverse IN A FEW SHORT STRIDES!
REMOVE THE GOO FROM THE JAR
AND FORM IT INTO A MONSTER SHAPE.
HAIR WILL GROW AND THE MONSTER WILL COME ALIVE WITHIN SIXTY SECONDS.

PLEASE STAND BACK TO AVOID BEING CRUSHED.

'Oh dear,' Neon said. 'You've only used a small bit of the goo, but I'm not sure what that'll mean – maybe we'll just get a monster foot or something. It'll be easy to clean up, don't worry.'

The two little unicorns exchanged worried glances as hair started to sprout from the goo.

'Here we go,' Neon said.

More and more hair grew – so much hair!

'When did you open this?' Neon asked.

The little unicorns shrugged. 'A minute ago?'

Eyes! Popping out of the goo and opening wide!

'It's definitely not a foot—' Neon began.

Moving arms!

She squinted at the thing in her hand. It was tiny and hairy and –

'FEED ME BRAINS!' it squeaked, brandishing a fist. 'FEED ME BRAINS!'

Neon quickly scanned the jar. The monster did resemble the picture, only it was a fraction of the size.

'FEED ME BRAINS!' the little monster screeched,

feed me brains!

before leaping from her hand and landing with the tiniest thud on the floor.

The little unicorns ran off screaming.

'FEED ME BRAINS! BRAINS! BRAINS! BRAINS!' It dragged its claws along Neon's ankle. It felt like being scratched by the bristles of a soft brush.

'Fearsome,' Neon said, rolling her eyes. 'Well, time to clean you up.' She raised her goo wand.

'FEED ME BRAINS!' the minuscule monster squeaked, before tearing off down the aisle at breakneck speed.

'Well, he's faster than I expected,' Neon said.

She heard a chuckle and turned to see the giant ghost rat hovering behind her.

'Don't laugh!' Neon said, struggling not to laugh herself.

'A minuscule brain-eating monster! And the customers thought I was bad!' the rat said. 'I like the little touches you're adding to the Goomart, Neon. Great fun!'

Neon smiled. She couldn't understand why anyone would want to clean up old Alaric.

12

The Strange Goo Society

When it was time for lunch, Neon and Geldie headed to the back room. But it wasn't any old back room. Every day, Old Lady Buck would use a different goo to spruce it up. Today she had used the MAGIC SPIDER WORLD IN THE SKY adventure goo.

'Wow,' Neon gasped as she opened the door to reveal thousands of glowing spiderwebs suspended in a twinkling starlit sky.

Geldie took a running jump and dived in. He bounced from cobweb to cobweb before taking his seat at one right in the middle. A large and strangely glamorous spider scuttled up and placed a tray of food in front of him.

Neon bounced in to join him, and received a matching tray of food.

Three large dead flies.

'Ugh!' she cried. 'I don't eat flies!'

'It's just the theme of the goo,' Geldie said. 'They're not real flies, they're just made to look like that. Once you bite into them, they'll taste like a normal meal. You have your starter fly, your main course fly and your dessert fly. The dessert is usually a chocolate mousse – it's amazing.'

'I keep thinking how different everything would be if I hadn't found the lipstick,' Neon said, gingerly biting into the first fly, to discover a nice cold luminous pink soup dripping into her mouth.

'The location of that lipstick was the biggest mystery of the UNIverse.' Geldie chuckled. 'Everyone's talking about you – you're famous now! The human who fell into our world with the last surviving portal opener. The news has spread way beyond Lumino.'

'So there were once more portal openers?' Neon said, biting into the next fly – it was lumpy and tasted like grapes in sunshine.

'Yes, a lot more,' Geldie said. 'Unicorns used them to

travel between the two worlds. But the human Unicorn Hunters got too close to uncovering our secret, so the Gooheads decided the safest thing was to destroy the portal openers. Then Greg made up the horse-with-a-horn thing, and finally our world was safe again. Now, if a Unicorn Hunter in the human world claims "a unicorn isn't a horse with a horn, they look just like us!" everyone laughs at them.'

'And unicorns just stopped searching for my portal opener?' Neon asked.

Geldie nodded. 'No human had used it, no unicorn had found it. They decided it must have ended up in a human bin.'

Talking about the lipstick made Neon think of home.

'How long did it take *you* to command goo?' she asked Geldie. 'And how many pots of goo do you think you needed?'

'Ten years and at least a thousand pots!' he chirped, before noticing Neon's face fall. 'I mean, well ... MUCH less time if you think of all the moments in those years when I was doing other things, like … sleeping … and … brushing my teeth.'

'I just don't believe I'll be able to command goo in *less than two days*,' Neon fretted. 'I'll only earn enough golds to buy one pot a day, and I'm going to need a lot more than that, aren't I?'

Geldie frowned. 'I think the Gooheads have set you an impossible task. It's like you were set up to fail.'

Neon slumped back in the cobweb and looked up at the enchanted sky. 'If I actually had goo to practise with, then maybe I could do it.'

Geldie lowered his voice to a whisper. 'Well, don't say I told you but there's always the Strange Goo Society.'

Neon sat up. 'Go on …'

'Normally goos are made in special factories and sold by permission of the Gooheads,' Geldie explained. 'But the Strange Goo Society brew whatever they want, whenever they want. They meet up and swap their brewed goos at a secret location. Rumour has it that there are always lots of goos to try out for free and play around with! If you could find their secret society, you'd be able to practise your commanding.'

'What?' Neon said. 'Geldie, this is exactly what I need!'

'Possibly,' he said, holding a hand up in caution. 'But their goos are not approved by the Gooheads. Technically, they could brew anything – you know, magical worlds you never come back from and that sort of thing.'

Neon gulped. 'So not like spider adventure goo then?'

Geldie shook his head gravely. 'It's a whole different level of goo.'

'Where does the Strange Goo Society meet?'

'They call it the Phantom Plaza,' Geldie said. 'The only problem is that no one knows where it is.'

'*Someone* must know,' Neon said.

'Only two kinds of beings know where to find the Phantom Plaza,' Geldie said. 'The unicorns in the Strange Goo Society.'

'And?' Neon pressed.

'And ghosts.'

13

Entire New Season Collection Goo!

Neon spent most of the afternoon thinking about the Strange Goo Society and how to find the Phantom Plaza. Occasionally, her mind wandered back to home and she shuddered thinking what her decoy in the human world was doing. Well, apart from saying 'I like rats' a lot.

And speaking of rats, she was hoping Alaric might pop up. He was a ghost and so he might know where to find the Phantom Plaza. But even though she heard the occasional customer scream, Alaric was nowhere to be seen.

At the end of the day, Old Lady Buck handed Neon her golds and she rushed out to meet Moya, who was sitting on one of the sparkly benches in the town square.

'I think we should go to Glittervoles to celebrate your first day,' Moya said. 'Before the sun sets and Scarlett Night begins.'

'YES!' Neon cried. She'd been desperate to see inside Glittervoles. 'But first I should buy a goo to practise my commanding.'

'You read my mind,' Moya said with a glint in her eye. 'Let's change our outfits into something *fancy.*'

The Slimy Wardrobe was about to close for the day, but Moya and Neon were just in time to pick up some new clothes goos. Moya went for a purple jumpsuit with glitter unicorn cuffs and Neon decided to spend some of her golds on a bargain goo called THE SLIMY WARDROBE'S ENTIRE NEW SEASON COLLECTION GOO.

She thought she was being sensible by buying lots of outfits for the price of one. But once again, she hadn't read the small print.

This bargain ENTIRE NEW SEASON GOO
allows you to wear each of the new season outfits
for around five uni-minutes at a time. The goo
will transform your outfit with a bang and some
dramatic smoke, racing through the whole
fabulous collection, wowing everyone!

They paid and made their way to Glittervoles.

'Ready?' Moya said, inspecting the instructions on her jar.

JUMPSUIT GOO WITH SPECTACULAR
SPARKLY UNICORN (THE GREG KIND)
CUFFS!
This is a one size fits all mega goo. No need to
measure the correct amount, simply pour on your
head for instant results.

Moya poured the contents on to her head and Neon watched in amazement as the silvery goo completely coated her, transforming her outfit into a jumpsuit with unicorn cuffs.

'WOAH!' Neon said. 'So cool!'

'Now you,' Moya said. 'I haven't heard of ENTIRE NEW SEASON COLLECTION goo, but it sounds like a bargain!'

Neon read the instructions. Like Moya's, it was a one size fits all goo that you poured on your head, so she figured at least this time she wouldn't have a wardrobe disaster like she did with the apron.

She poured the contents on her head and suddenly all of Lumino went blurry. There was a loud *BANG* and when she looked down she was wearing a twinkling technicolour lace gown.

'I did it!' Neon cheered. 'I commanded the goo!'

Moya linked arms with Neon. '*Now* we're ready for Glittervoles.'

14

Glittervoles

Inside, Glittervoles was heaving with unicorns all dressed in wildly bright clothing with equally bright stripes of hair. There was a red glow about the place because of the windows, which were covered in red slime Scarlett Night decorations.

'Now, let's see if we can get our table, I did book one,' Moya said. 'Just need to find Suzette …'

Much to Neon's amazement a squirrel with sprinkles for fur bounced from shoulder to shoulder through the crowd and landed at their feet.

'Moya!' it cried. 'And, oh! Is this the human?'

'Yep!' Moya said. 'Neon, this is Suzette. Suzette, this is Neon.'

'You're a squirrel!' Neon cried. 'Made of sprinkles!'

'And you have eyes!' the little squirrel said, leaning

on her paws and looking up at Neon dreamily. 'We're learning so much about each other already!'

There was a *BANG*.

The whole place fell silent, and a fabric-smelling smoke wafted up Neon's nose.

'Oh!' Suzette said, coughing a little. 'Your outfit changed! Did you get THE SLIMY WARDROBE'S ENTIRE NEW SEASON COLLECTION GOO?'

Neon could feel her cheeks getting hot with embarrassment.

She looked down and her technicolour lace gown had been replaced with a rainbow knit cropped jacket and sequined shorts.

'NOTHING TO SEE HERE!' Suzette shouted. 'JUST A HUMAN WHO HAS PURCHASED A VERY ATTENTION-GRABBING GOO!'

The hustle and bustle started up again and everyone got back to their conversations.

Neon frantically scanned the jar. 'Is my outfit going to keep doing that?'

'Just for a few hours, then it'll wear off,' Suzette said.

'It's a bargain though, because when you get home, you'll find the whole collection hanging in your wardrobe. Good choice! Now, let's get you your complimentary Volefizz.'

Neon looked around and in every glass there was a little luminous vole, swimming in excited circles and causing the drink to bubble and froth.

'A-a-are the voles real?' Neon stuttered as she leaned forward and prodded a glass on the nearest table.

'You're not suggesting I make *fake* Volefizz are you?' Suzette asked.

She guided them to a table and then ran off to get their drinks and a menu. In the corner, Neon spotted a familiar face – it was Filly Spangle. She was shaking the jukebox and shouting, 'MICE GURLS! I WANT TO LISTEN TO THE MICE GURLS!'

Up at the bar, waiters and waitresses with rainbow mohawks were returning the empty glasses, allowing the voles to jump out into an ice bath to get ready for the next drink.

'What do the voles do?' Neon asked.

'They make the fizz, of course!' the squirrel said as she reappeared with two Volefizzes.

'Oh, like the fizz in soda,' Neon said as she leaned forward and watched the vole at work in her glass.

'NO! Not like anything human,' cried Suzette. 'This is a fizz like you've never tasted before.'

'Cheers,' Moya said to Neon, before turning to her vole. 'And cheers to you too!'

The vole saluted her.

Neon lifted the glass to her lips and the vole swam to the side and leaned back, like a human lazing in a Jacuzzi. She squeezed her eyes shut and took a sip.

The feeling was overwhelming and instant. It felt like she'd eaten ten thousand packets of popping candy. It felt like there were BEES in her mouth. It felt like an entire collection of Irish dancers were kicking her teeth.

'Delicious, isn't it?' Suzette oozed. 'Now, I'll give you a moment to look at the menu – I highly recommend the Glitter Chunk Platter.'

'Neon!' came a cry, and much to her delight she

saw Geldie making his way towards them.

'It's your friend from the Goomart! Come and join us,' Moya said, rushing off to get another chair.

'And what about your food?' Suzette asked, holding a heart-shaped order pad in her sprinkle paws.

'We'll all have the same,' Moya called. 'Three of your finest sparkle burgers, thanks, Suzette.'

'And how would you like your sparkle burgers cooked?'

'Bright, please,' Moya said.

'Luminous, please,' Geldie said.

They turned to Neon.

'Um, well done?' Neon said quietly.

'Well done for what?' Suzette asked. 'Oh, is this a human thing?'

'She'll have it bright, like me,' Moya said. 'And we'll have some rainbow fries to share.'

'Coming right up!' Suzette cried, before racing off.

'She's a *squirrel* made of *sprinkles*,' Neon said in disbelief. There was a *BANG* and the whole place jumped.

'Sorry,' Neon said sheepishly. She was now wearing sequined dungarees with glowing pockets. 'Next time I'm going to get a *normal* outfit.'

The sparkle burger was delicious, and Neon, Moya and Geldie laughed and joked as they ate and discussed all the different kinds of goo.

BANG!

It wasn't just the unicorns who jumped every time Neon's outfit changed. Every vole did too – flying up in the air, then splashing down in their drinks and making a mess.

Neon looked up at the artsy splatter-print hat now sitting on her head, complete with a neon-pink veil.

'Oooh,' Moya said, taking a sip of her drink. 'You suit a hat.'

Suzette scuttled past them, mopping up some Volefizz. 'Don't worry about Volefizz spilling everywhere,' she said, spotting Neon's embarrassed expression. 'You look FABULOUS!'

'I just wish it wouldn't make such a bang,' Neon said with a cough. 'And that it didn't also come with dramatic smoke effects.'

She looked over to the corner to see Filly Spangle still hanging out by the jukebox. She seemed to be alone.

'Should we invite her over?' Neon asked.

'I'm not sure she'd like that,' Moya said. 'She goes to my school and doesn't have any friends. She seems to like it that way.'

'She was shouting something earlier about a mice song?' Neon said.

'Mice Gurls!' Moya cheered. 'Only one of the most popular bands in the UNIverse.'

'One of their songs is playing right now,' Geldie said. 'Listen.'

They were singing 'IF YOU WANNA BE MY CHEESE'.

'You know,' Neon said, 'they remind me a lot of a band called the Spice Girls in the human world.'

'I bet the Spice Girls aren't nearly as good as the Mice Gurls,' Geldie said. 'The Mice Gurls are all very cool and unique – there's Scary Mouse and Sporty Mouse, Baby Mouse and Posh Mouse and finally—'

'Let me guess,' Neon said. 'Ginger Mouse?'

Geldie looked confused. 'No. He's called Jerry.'

Neon watched as Filly Spangle danced around on her own.

'She mostly keeps to herself at school,' Moya whispered. 'There was a rumour going round that she's a member of the Strange Goo Society. It's this secret society that—'

Neon gasped. 'Filly Spangle knows where the Phantom Plaza is?!'

Moya looked puzzled. 'Wait, how do you know about that?'

Geldie raised a hand. 'I might've mentioned that it's a place with lots of goos to play with.'

'I could practise commanding goo,' Neon explained to Moya. 'If I could find a way in.'

They all looked curiously at Filly Spangle.

'I guess the big question is,' Moya whispered, 'would she tell you how to get there?'

BANG!

Everyone jumped.

Neon's outfit transformed into a pair of spotted green leggings and a simple T-shirt with *THE SLIMY WARDROBE IS COOL* stamped on it. The letters started flashing.

'Ugh, this was a bad choice of goo,' Neon groaned, as everyone turned to look at her again.

15

Uni-Taxis and the Hunt for Filly Spangle

Glittervoles was closing early, in line with the Scarlett Night rules. As the glowing blue sun set, there was a mad dash among the diners to pay their bills and race home.

But Neon was distracted. She'd lost track of Filly Spangle and was desperately trying to spot her in the shrinking Glittervoles crowd.

'I need to speak to her,' Neon said to Moya and Geldie. 'Tonight.'

'But it's Scarlett Night, Neon,' Moya said. 'We have to get home where it's safe.'

'But I'm almost out of time,' Neon protested.

'She's right,' Geldie said. 'There's no time to lose.'

The Glittervoles staff began ushering them out,

but Filly Spangle had gone.

'CLOSING TIME! SCARLETT NIGHT!'

'Maybe she's in the back?' Moya said.

'EVERYONE OUT!'

'You go on, I'll meet you at home,' Neon said, squeezing through the crowd to where Suzette was cleaning tables.

'Have you seen Filly Spangle?'

'She's already left, I'm afraid,' Suzette said. 'She got a uni-taxi home.'

'A uni-taxi?'

'Yes,' Suzette said. 'Would you like me to call one for you?'

Neon nodded.

'And here,' Suzette said, handing Neon a Glitter Chunk Platter. 'You'll need this – uni-taxis like to be paid in good food.'

Neon wasn't sure what a uni-taxi looked like, but what arrived was beyond anything she could have imagined.

It was a vehicle, because it had wheels, but it also looked a lot like a giant fake unicorn – the Greg kind.

A cheery man lifted a panel in the fake unicorn's head. 'Where to?'

'Filly Spangle's house?' Neon asked hopefully.

'Delighted to take you there! Hop in!' the driver said.

Much to Neon's surprise, a compartment opened in the body and glittering steps unrolled in front of her.

Inside, there was a comfy shimmering seat, and a lever that lifted the fake unicorn's glittery tail so she could peek out of the back.

Neon watched the bright lights of Lumino flash by. She looked at her watch – she had until midnight, when Scarlett would arrive. She tapped her foot nervously. She still had time …

It began to rain and Neon snuggled back in her seat as technicolour raindrops pelted the windows. But quickly, and without warning, the clouds turned blood red.

'Little Lumino is just up ahead,' came the driver's voice through a speaker in the cabin.

Neon peered out at the village, nestled among glowing gold trees.

Moments later, she was staring up at the tall gates of the Spangle house as the uni-taxi tore off back to the city.

'What am I doing?' she whispered.

BANG! Her outfit changed to a candy-cane striped skirt and matching slouchy shirt.

'Could you stop that now, goo?' she pleaded, even though the goo almost certainly couldn't hear her.

'SOMETHING IS ON FIRE ON THE DRIVEWAY!' came a squeal. 'I SEE SMOKE!'

'I'LL CHECK,' came Filly's voice in reply, followed by doors banging and hurried footsteps.

'Argh,' Neon said, trying to bat away the smoke from her outfit. 'Why can't I just be *normal*? Even in the UNIverse I'm weird!'

'You've got that right,' Filly said.

Neon waited for Filly to open the gates and let her in, but she just stood there, arms folded.

'What?' Filly said. 'It's Scarlett Night, you're meant to be at home. Did you not get the memo?'

'I have an urgent question,' Neon said. 'I was wondering if you could point me in the direction of the Phantom Plaza?'

Filly coughed. 'What?'

'The Phantom Plaza,' Neon said again. 'I'm running out of time to practise commanding goo, and I thought maybe the Strange Goo Society could help me.'

'I don't know what that is,' Filly said, turning to leave.

'Please,' Neon said, grabbing hold of the gates. 'I just want to go home to my world.'

Filly swivelled on her heel without saying anything, then marched over and pressed a button by the gates. Neon expected them to open, but instead a man's voice rang out.

'Uni-taxis?'

'Yes, I need a taxi immediately, for a Neon Gallup,' Filly said.

'Oh no, don't send me away!' Neon pleaded.

The same uni-taxi came to a screeching halt next to her.

'Where to now?' the driver asked.

'Please, Filly,' Neon said. 'It's really important that I—'

'Whiskers & Gloop,' Filly said to the driver.

Neon did a double take. 'Wait – what?'

'Just get in,' Filly ordered. 'And go to the fish tanks. You'll need to test the water to make sure it's *just right*.'

'Whiskers & Gloop is the pet shop,' Neon said.

Filly leaned closer and whispered, 'Or is it?'

16

Whiskers & Gloop

'Neon!' the driver pleaded through the intercom. 'Stop messing with the uni-taxi tail!'

'Sorry!' Neon excitedly flipped the tail lever one final time before they veered left and halted outside Whiskers & Gloop. She was going to the Phantom Plaza!

She jumped out of the uni-taxi and ran to the window. She could see jars of goo and bowls of goo and baskets of goo and fish tanks of goo.

A little bell trilled as she opened the fluffy door.

'We're closing in two minutes,' the old man at the counter said. 'Scarlett Night.'

Neon nodded.

'You looking for a pet? Just got some nice Mystery Pet goos in – and this time I think we've got a few dinosaurs.'

'Dinosaurs?' Neon said. 'Aren't they extinct?'

The old man looked confused. 'They thought about bannin' them, if that's what you mean. Some unicorns were lookin' for a small pet like a hamster and were quite upset when the goo made a life-size stegosaurus. You can't fit them in a hamster cage, and some even try to eat your relatives. Anyway, they didn't make them extinct – whatever that is – but the Gooheads put a warnin' on them. Now it says, THIS MYSTERY PET GOO MIGHT MAKE A DINOSAUR.'

'I'm just looking for a fish tank,' Neon said.

'*Oh … right.* Gotcha,' the shopkeeper said and waved his hand towards the back of the shop. 'Be my guest.'

Neon walked slowly to the fish tanks filled with goo and stared at them. *You'll need to test the water.* There was a chance Filly Spangle was playing a prank on her, but with absolutely nothing to lose, except perhaps her dignity, Neon leaned over one of the tanks and stuck her head in. She had expected goo up her nose, but the transition was seamless – it was like slipping past a curtain.

She couldn't believe it! She was somewhere else – somewhere ghostly and watery. There were unicorns

there, but they were ghostly and watery too. Neon looked down. Her body was missing!

'A THOUSAND UNICORN WELCOMES!' a little man cried, pulling Neon through. Weirdly, she felt her feet leave the floor of Whiskers & Gloop.

Neon's jaw, or the ghostly, barely there version of it, was practically on the floor. All around her floated outlines of unicorns, swapping goos and laughing. Above her head floated goo jars galore, going up and up and disappearing into a dripping goo ceiling.

'Anyone want to swap me for one of my Beard goos?' a unicorn cried. 'The wise beard goo and angry beard goo are the best.'

'Oh, no thank you,' Neon said. She drifted past. There were ghostly *bangs* and puffs of glitter as unicorns happily activated the contents of the jars. She had no idea what she was looking for, anything to practise on, really, just maybe not something that would mean she'd arrive for work with a beard she couldn't explain.

'I've got Strange goos!'

'Want my Dangerous goos? I'll swap for a

Forbidden Prank goo!'

'Risk your life in a banned Adventure goo! I tried it and it was GREAT! I only lost four fingers!'

Neon gave that one a swerve.

'THE PLAZA WILL BE CLOSING IN FIFTEEN MINUTES, DUE TO SCARLETT NIGHT SAFETY MEASURES. THIS IS YOUR REMINDER TO PLEASE NOT OPEN ANY GOOS THAT WILL TRANSPORT YOU TO TEMPORARY GOO WORLDS, BECAUSE YOU ARE UNLIKELY TO GET BACK IN TIME. DOING SO WILL RESULT IN AN IMMEDIATE BAN.'

Neon stopped next to a quiet old unicorn with her head in a book.

IMAGI-UNI GOOS read a slimy sign floating above her head.

'Excuse me,' Neon whispered. 'What is an Imagi-uni goo?'

The old woman snapped the book closed and pulled a bottle of multicoloured goo from her pocket. 'My speciality! It takes you to the place of your imagination and makes it real! Brewed using an ancient recipe passed down through generations of my family.'

'Wow,' Neon said, taking the bottle. 'This is perfect.' She had come to the Phantom Plaza to practise her commanding, but maybe she could use the Imagi-uni goo to get home! She'd just have to imagine her bedroom and the goo would make it real. A shortcut!

'What have you got to swap?' the old woman asked.

'Oh,' Neon said with a sad smile. 'Nothing.' She reluctantly handed the bottle back.

The old woman thought for a moment before handing the bottle to Neon. 'Take it, dear,' she said kindly. 'Enjoy it.'

Neon squealed with unrestrained delight and popped the lid off.

'Wait—' the old woman cried, but Neon had already scooped out the contents. The goo leaped from her hand and floated in front of her, twisting and stretching.

An alarm sounded.

'You shouldn't have opened it tonight!' the woman cried. 'Didn't anyone tell you not to use goo that transports you to other worlds on Scarlett Night? You'll be banned from The Phantom Plaza now!'

The plaza started to darken. Everything turned grey, then streaks of black shot across Neon's vision.

'EMERGENCY! SPILT STRANGE GOO, EVERY-ONE REPORT TO THE EXIT! THE PHANTOM PLAZA IS NOW CLOSED! EMERGENCY!'

The unicorns began to move towards the gooey ceiling, but Neon couldn't budge.

'I'm sorry,' the old woman said. 'You'll have to go with the Imagi-uni goo. I hope your imagination doesn't take you too far ...' And with that, she shot up and out of sight.

Neon looked around frantically for help, but every-one was disappearing through the ceiling.

Black goo swelled up around her, strapping her arms to her sides.

'Welcome to your Imagi-uni goo!' came a voice in Neon's ear. 'Please keep your arms, legs, brain and other important items inside the goo barrier at all times.'

'HELP!' Neon cried. But it was too late – her stomach lurched, the Phantom Plaza disappeared, and she was plunged into darkness.

17

Scarlett, the Villain Goo!

When Neon came to, she was furious with herself for being so impulsive.

But there wasn't time to dwell on it. Not where she'd landed …

Around her, dripping goo hung dark and stringy like tattered ghosts. She looked up to see a starlit sky with flying rats with angel wings.

Much to her annoyance, it definitely wasn't her bedroom.

A rat swooped low and began flying in circles around her head.

So this was where her imagination had taken her. *Great*.

'I wanted to go home!' she shouted at the winged rats. They stuck their noses in the air and carried on with their business of flying back and forth, occasionally stopping for a breather.

Neon plonked herself down on the gooey floor and put her head in her hands.

'How do I even get out of here?' she grumbled to no one. 'How long does a transportation goo last?'

'Depends on the goo, really. Some have exit doors. Others you just have to wait for the goo to fade. And some are designed never to let anyone out.'

Neon looked up to see the ghostly outline of Alaric.

'Are these meant to be me?' he said, pointing at the winged angel rats with one paw and clutching his heart with the other. 'The flattery!'

'I think there have just been a lot of rodents in my life recently,' Neon said wearily. 'You, Suzette, the voles, my parents' cafe, Ratty's, which is rat-themed.'

'Wonderful!' Alaric said. 'Your parents sound delightful!'

'What are you doing here, Alaric?' she asked. Whatever the reason, she was relieved to see a familiar face.

'Oh, you know, we ghosts can float through anything, even goo worlds. I happened to hear that a little human in the Phantom Plaza had activated a goo to another world, and I just wanted to check she was all right.'

Neon was about to insist she was fine, when everything turned crimson red.

Suddenly, she didn't feel so fine any more.

'What's happening?' she said, getting to her feet.

'Oh no,' Alaric said, floating closer to her, as if he – a ghost unable to move anything – might be able to protect her. 'Ghost goos like me can travel freely through any part of the UNIverse,' he paused. 'And, unfortunately, a certain villain goo can too …'

A cackle rang out around them. Red lightning struck the sky.

'You don't mean—?' Neon began, just as a huge gloopy figure strode through the hanging goo. She had claws and a gooey face. Her hair was frizzy and furious and burned at the edges. And her long red cloak swished like a pendulum as she walked, as though it was counting down the seconds to disaster.

'Scarlett,' Neon whispered in terror as the villain goo stalked right past them.

'*Phew*, she hasn't noticed us,' Alaric whispered.

At that, Scarlett snapped her head to the side and came to an abrupt halt.

Neon gulped.

Slowly, the villain goo turned and fixed her red eyes on Neon.

'Whoooo aaaarrrreeee yoooou?' came Scarlett's raspy drawl as she grew closer. 'Haaaaang oooon,' she added, before coughing.

Neon stared at her.

'WHO ARE YOU?' Scarlett bellowed, her voice booming and powerful and completely different to the voice that had come before it.

'She's a villain goo, so she can

do all the villain voices,' Alaric explained, noticing Neon's confused expression.

'I'm, um, Neon,' Neon said, her voice wobbling. 'Just ignore me though, I'm not even meant to be here. Not in this goo, and not even in the UNIverse, actually! I'm a human, so you can leave me alone.'

Scarlett moved closer still, until she was towering over Neon. She was at least three times her height.

'A human, you say?'

Neon nodded. 'I fell into the UNIverse by accident. I found a portal opener. It was an old lipstick.' She laughed nervously. 'Silly me!'

Scarlett's eyes narrowed. 'This is different.'

'Different?' Neon asked, trying her best to smile, though she was shaking so much she could hear her toenails clacking.

'Yes, different,' Scarlett said with a fiendish grin. 'Yeeees.'

Neon braced herself for an attack. She remembered Moya's dad saying no unicorn who tried to clean up Scarlett lived to tell the tale. Neon decided she was definitely going to die.

But to her surprise, Scarlett threw her hands in the air in delight.

'This is it! At last, I have found my story – something worthy of the UNIverse's most notorious villain goo!'

'What?' Neon whispered.

'YES!' Scarlett roared. 'A NEMESIS! A *HUMAN* ONE THAT HAS TRAVELLED ALL THE WAY TO THE UNIverse TO STOP ME—'

'Uh, I didn't do that,' Neon said, but Scarlett wasn't listening.

'IN MY STORY, WE WILL BATTLE SO SHE CAN SAVE THE UNIverse FROM DESTRUCTION. BUT I AM ALL-POWERFUL – I WANT TO DESTROY THE UNIverse *AND* I WANT THE LIPSTICK TO OPEN THE PORTAL TO THE HUMAN WORLD, SO I CAN DESTROY THEM AS WELL!'

'Oh, unicorns,' Neon said, realising what she'd done. She'd given Scarlett a purpose – and a terrible, terrible plan.

Scarlett began spinning in giddy circles.

'I think that's a *terrible* idea,' Neon tried, hoping that might work. 'And it would be a rubbish story.'

Scarlett grinned broadly. 'HAND THE LIPSTICK OVER NOW OR FACE MY VILLAINOUS WRATH!'

'I can't,' Neon said. 'It got confiscated by the Gooheads and they're not going to give it—'

She was interrupted by a flash of red light. Scarlett roared with fury as the wind picked up and whipped itself into a frenzied hurricane. Neon screamed as she was lifted off her feet. The sinister red stars in the sky fell around her, smashing to the ground like glass.

'Alaric!' she cried. 'HELP!'

'CRY FOR HELP ALL YOU LIKE,' Scarlett cackled. 'NOTHING CAN SAVE YOU NOW, LITTLE HUMAN!'

Red flashes shot past Neon and the goo began to warp, forming the face of Scarlett – only this time she was ten times bigger than before!

'MWAHAHAHAHA!' she laughed.

Scarlett opened her huge goo mouth to reveal spiked

red teeth. Goo wrapped around Neon, pulling her closer to the terrifying jaws.

'Alaric!' Neon shrieked. 'Alaric!'

She felt two paws grab her shoulders, and then everything went dark.

SQUELCH! BANG!

Neon felt herself landing with a thud on hard ground. She looked up.

She was back in Whiskers & Gloop!

She quickly got to her feet and stuck her head back in the fish tank – she was sure the paws she'd felt were Alaric's, but was that even possible?

Her face slipped through the slime and she could see the empty Phantom Plaza.

'Alaric?' she cried.

The ghost rat limped into view. His eyelids were drooping and he flinched when he moved, as if he were in pain.

'Alaric? What's wrong?'

'Ghost goos can only touch real things if we try very hard. Pulling you to safety took all my strength.'

Neon tried to dive back in, but the goo bounced her out again!

'Looks like you're banned,' the shopkeeper said.

A red trickle of goo began to seep from the tank. It snaked around the floor as if looking for something. Or some*one*.

'Scarlett!' Neon screamed.

BANG!

The Slimy Wardrobe goo finally wore off and she was back in her oversized Goomart apron. She tried to lift it like a skirt to run, but she tripped and fell to her knees.

Red goo began to pool around her.

'Neon!'

She looked up to see Geldie outside the shop.

'You've got to get home!' he yelled through the window. 'I've been looking everywhere for you!'

'SHE'S HERE!' Neon shouted. 'SCARLETT'S HERE!' She scurried out of Whiskers & Gloop as fast as she could, accidentally smacking Geldie in the face with the furry door as she went. He fell backwards and hit the ground with a thud.

'RUN, GELDIE! COME ON!' she called back as she did a wobble-run in her oversized apron all the way to the McGlows' house.

She fell through the door and collapsed on the unicorn-patterned carpet.

It took her a moment to realise Geldie wasn't with her.

18

Goomartastrophy!

'Neon!' Moya whispered, sliding down the banister and landing on her friend.

'Ow,' Neon groaned from under Moya's unicorn dressing gown.

'It's the middle of the night! I didn't want to tell my parents you weren't at home in case they told the Gooheads and you got in trouble. So I said you were hiding under the bed because you were scared of Scarlett. Where have you *been*? Geldie stayed out to try and find you!'

Neon didn't know where to start, so she started with Geldie.

'Oh no!' Moya said, grabbing Neon's arm and pulling her upstairs. On the landing was a telephone shaped like a Greg unicorn.

Moya began frantically dialling, looking around to check her parents hadn't woken up.

'Hello, Whiskers & Gloop? Yes, sorry, I know it's very late and you're closed. I'm looking for Geldie O'Splendid. I believe he was hit in the face with a door? Yes … Ah, OK. I see … uh-huh …'

Neon widened her eyes at Moya, hoping for some sign that Geldie hadn't been eaten by Scarlett. But Moya was deep in conversation.

'Oh, really? Gosh! Uh-huh … uh-huh … No thanks, I don't really like dinosaurs. OK, goodbye.'

She hung up the phone.

'Well?' Neon pressed.

'So, *apparently*, they had to put a warning on the mystery pet goos because people were buying them hoping for a small creature like a hamster, but they were getting dinosaurs instead.'

Neon put her head in her hands. 'About Geldie, Moya. What did they say about *Geldie*?'

'Oh! Yes. Geldie was collected by an ambulance and whisked off to safety. Apparently, his face looked a little sore, but he'll be fine.'

Neon practically collapsed with relief. But Geldie wasn't all she had to worry about. She told Moya all about the Phantom Plaza and Scarlett.

As she was telling her story, a bright blue sun rose in the sky. It was a new day.

'Don't worry,' Moya said, to the sound of birds chirping outside. 'You survived Scarlett Night. She won't be back for a whole year. Now, you'd better get ready for work.You'll need those golds to get that goo!'

'But what about the lipstick? What if Scarlett went to the Gooheads to find it?' Neon fretted.

'Trust me, Neon, if that happened, we'd know about it,' Moya said, sounding not at all worried. 'She only comes around once a year.'

'But I'm her nemesis now. Don't you think Scarlett will be waiting for me in the Goomart? To EAT ME?'

'Eat you?' Moya said cheerily. 'Nah! Scarlett Night comes and goes, and she comes and goes with it. That's why it's called Scarlett Night, not Scarlett *Week* or Scarlett *Month*. You have *nothing* to worry about.'

Neon arrived at the Goomart in her gigantic apron.

'Geldie?' she called out hopefully, but the checkout was empty. 'GELDIE?'

'Oh, he's not well. Got hit in the face with a door. So Old Lady Buck called me in as a backup.'

Neon turned round slowly.

'Filly Spangle?' she said in disbelief.

'Filly was waiting outside, right before we opened up,' Lady Buck said as she breezed past. 'Wonderful coincidence!'

'You set me up!' Neon growled. 'I nearly DIED in the Phantom Plaza. You were hoping I wouldn't come back so you could have this Goomart job! And now you've got Geldie's job instead!'

Filly narrowed her eyes and stepped closer. 'I was helping you. And I'm only helping Old Lady Buck because Geldie's injured – because of *you*, Neon.'

'I don't believe you,' Neon said.

Filly Spangle's face fell. 'Well … I don't care!' she

said and swiftly marched away up the aisle.

'Another glorious gooey day!' Old Lady Buck said, handing a furious-looking Neon her goo wand. 'Let's get to work.'

Neon didn't care about lunch or whatever fun Adventure goo had been unleashed in the back room that day. All she wanted was to say sorry to Geldie and make sure he was all right.

Moya arrived with a shopping list from her mum, and Neon helped her fill her basket.

'I can't be long,' Neon said. 'I'm going to see Geldie on my lunch break, to check he's OK. Where does he live?'

'In Little Trot,' Moya said. 'You won't be able to get there and back on your lunch break. It's too far.'

Neon frowned and plonked a UNI-CONES WITH EXTRA WHIP AND NEIGH goo in the basket.

'I'm sure he's fine. He probably just needed a day off to rearrange his face,' Moya said.

'It's a good thing he's off work,' Filly said, stalking past them with her goo wand. 'I'm much more efficient. I've manned the tills *and* cleaned up that annoying ghost rat.'

Neon felt like *she'd* been hit in the face with a door.

'Alaric?' she whispered, hoping with all her heart that Filly meant some *other* ghost rat.

'Oh, was that his name?' Filly said. 'I can't believe you didn't do it on your first day – he's so slow and sluggish, it was easy!'

Neon felt her stomach drop, and her knees dropped with it. She hit the cold floor with a bang.

'Neon!' Moya cried, bending down to help her up.

'No,' Neon whispered, tears streaming down her face. 'He can't be gone.'

'It was just *so* easy,' Filly said again, not noticing how upset Neon was.

Neon's mind was racing. If Alaric hadn't saved her, he wouldn't have been so tired and easy to clean up. If Neon hadn't hit Geldie in the face with the door, Filly

Spangle wouldn't have been there to clean him up in the first place! She turned to Moya. 'It's all my fault!' she wailed. 'In every possible way!'

Filly Spangle looked confused. 'It's got nothing to do with you, Neon. I'm just *really* good at cleaning up.'

19

So Long, Alaric

Neon walked around the Goomart with her over-sized apron trailing along the ground and her shoulders sagging sadly.

She spent most of the day searching the aisles for a GIANT GHOST RAT goo so she could bring him back, until Old Lady Buck told her they didn't stock it any more.

'That's a vintage goo,' she explained. 'Plus, it took him about fifty years to learn how to speak to us. You'll never be able to recreate Alaric, I'm afraid.'

So instead, Neon spent her earnings on a FUNERAL OUTFIT goo from the Slimy Wardrobe, which, annoyingly, was a bright green dress that cried and spurted tears from the pockets and shoulders.

That evening, she gathered everyone in aisle five, where she'd first met Alaric, for a memorial service. It was surprising how many customers showed up. There were at least a hundred unicorns there.

'FEED ME BRAINS!'

'Shush,' Neon said to the little monster gnawing at her ankle.

She took a deep breath.

'Alaric was a giant ghost rat. He was the finest ghost rat in town. All of you met him, some of you benefited from his shopping tips.'

A lot of unicorns nodded. Many of them dabbed tears from their eyes.

'He was not only a wonderful ghost and very large rodent, he was also a special part of the UNIverse. He saved my life and he made me laugh. He was a great rat and he was a great friend.'

'A very nice tribute!' Old Lady Buck said. 'He would have adored it.'

Neon's dad's words echoed in her head: *It's about time someone was nice about rats!*

She wished more than anything that she could go home and tell him what a wonderful idea Ratty's Cafe was.

20

Neon's Birthday!

Zero days until Neon's tenth birthday

The night before her birthday, Neon had the strangest dream. She saw Scarlett soaring menacingly above Goohead Central while a flying choir of angel rats sang the words, *BE VERY AFRAID, LITTLE UNICORN* to the tune of 'Don't Be Afraid, Little Unicorn'.

Neon woke with a start, her pyjamas soaked with sweat. She peeked between the curtains and was sure she saw a red tint on the rising sun. Thoughts of the villain goo were so distracting, for a moment she'd forgotten it was her birthday.

Downstairs, the McGlows had got her a special BIRTHDAY BREAKFAST CAKE goo – a cake that burped up breakfast items, like glow-in-the-dark

146

pancakes that shouted 'HAPPY BIRTHDAY!' in a different language every time you took a bite.

'*Feliz cumpleaños!*'

'*Bon anniversaire!*'

'*Buon compleanno!*'

'*Wszystkiego najlepszego!*'

'*С Днём рождения!*'

But as nice as it was, now that her birthday had arrived, any hope of commanding goo was slipping away forever. Neon had never felt so sad. She was so deflated she didn't even pick up her wand at the Goomart that day.

Roller-skating vampires sailed past her and singing cakes splodged along the aisles past her feet. The shelves sprouted colourful unicorn fruits and dripped with smelly cheese.

'OH MY UNICORNS!' Old Lady Buck cried.

She stood in the doorway of the Goomart with her jaw practically on the floor.

'LOOK AT THE MESS! I KNEW I SHOULDN'T HAVE GONE TO THE HAIRDRESSER'S!'

Neon noticed her hair had been dyed and was now covered in colourful unicorns – the horse kind, the Greg kind.

'WE NEED BACKUP!' she roared. 'SERIOUS BACKUP.' And then she tore off down the street crying, 'SUZETTE!'

Neon sighed. She'd ruined the Goomart. She'd ruined everything.

'NEON!' came a shout, and she saw Moya and Geldie racing towards her. Geldie's face had a bandage on it.

Oh yeah, and she'd maimed Geldie with a door.

'I'm the worst,' she groaned.

Moya shook her arm. 'Neon, we have news about Scarlett! She's—'

Her words were swallowed up by lightning cracking outside. The three of them ran to the window just in time to see the sky turn blood red.

Geldie whimpered. 'She stuck around! She's changed her pattern for the first time! It's all over the news!'

'THE GOOHEADS!' Neon cried. 'THE LIPSTICK!'

Neon grabbed her goo wand and a basket and ran

along the shelves, scooping random jars into it. 'I'll pay you back, it's an emergency!' she shouted, even though Old Lady Buck had left the building. Then she tore out of the door and down the street, all the way to Goohead Central …

21

Gooheads in Danger!

Even from outside, Neon could tell something was *very* wrong at Goohead Central.

The gooey sign that hung on the building was sliding its way down to the pavement like it had died, and someone had drawn a silly moustache on the Greg statue.

Bright light seeped out from the cracks around the doors, and when Neon pulled them open, she was blinded by flashes of telltale red.

Moya and Geldie caught up with her and stared at the new red walls and windows of Goohead Central in horror.

'Oh no,' Moya said.

'Scarlett is a villain *and* a vandal!' Geldie scoffed, pointing madly at the moustache on the Greg statue.

'The moustache is the least of our worries,' Neon said gravely. She hoisted the Goomart basket higher on her arm and tightened her grip on her goo wand.

'You're not planning to go in there, are you? With this random assortment of goo?' Geldie asked, picking up one of the jars from the basket and inspecting it. 'Especially this Discount Skeleton Ballet goo.'

'I have to,' Neon said, stepping forward into the red abyss. 'I can't let her get the lipstick!'

The three of them crept along the corridor, with Moya talking really loudly and Geldie wincing at every word.

'I just can't believe she's back already!' Moya said. 'Do you think she lost her diary or something?'

'Shhhhh,' Geldie whispered. 'She might *hear* you.'

'She's only here because I gave her a purpose,' Neon said, forging on ahead. 'Finally she's a villain with a storyline, and it's all my fault.'

They reached the door to the Gooheads' room. Neon began handing jars of goo to the others.

'We have to stop her.'

'Neon,' Moya said slowly. 'This is MILD CHEESE goo. I don't think it can stop a supervillain …'

Geldie whimpered, then brandished a jar of DISCOUNT ICE LOLLY goo, and together they kicked the door open.

It hit the wall with a *bang*. A sinister cackle rang out around them.

On the half-moon table, where the Gooheads had once sat, there was now only a gooey villain.

A gooey villain HOLDING A VERY IMPORTANT LIPSTICK!

'That's *my* lipstick,' Neon growled.

'Where are the Gooheads?' Moya said, racing over and ducking under the table. 'I can't see them anywhere!'

Scarlett stared at her with an amused look. She reached down slowly and grabbed Moya by the leg.

'Nice shoes. Once I destroy the UNIverse, I will wear—'

'Aw, thank you!' Moya interrupted. 'I got them half price at the Slimy Wardrobe.'

Scarlett paused.

'It's not a good idea to interrupt a villain's evil monologue,' she said.

'I just thought you might want to know where to buy a pair,' Moya said.

Neon edged around the room, her eyes darting about as she tried to formulate a plan to get the lipstick.

'Ah!' Scarlett said, flashing red. 'The human. She's here to stop me.'

'NOW!' Neon cried, grabbing her jar of goo and ripping the lid off.

Geldie, however, didn't seem to understand the urgency of the situation as he carefully and *very* slowly removed his goo and held it while it transformed into a dripping ice lolly.

'Discount Ice Lolly goo,' he said with a groan as the remnants trickled down his wrist. 'Discounted because it's already melted.'

He brandished the lolly stick at Scarlett, like the worst ever sword.

The villain goo just laughed. 'Is that all you've got?'

Neon stared down at the goo in her hand.

GLITTER SLIDE GOO.

She stared at the label. There were no instructions!

She had no idea what a Glitter Slide goo was, but she instinctively began stretching it in her hands and swinging it around her head, just like Old Lady Buck had done with the 3-IN-1 PICNIC goo. To her surprise, it began fizzing. Glitter rained down on them, sticking to Scarlett's gooey exterior until she was practically glowing with sparkles.

'The goo is working! I'm commanding it!' Neon shouted.

Scarlett growled and charged, soaring through the air with a flying kick.

'She knows every mode of combat!' Geldie cried. 'Watch out, Neon!'

Neon ducked as more glitter rained from the ceiling. If she wasn't being attacked by an evil villain, the whole effect would have been magical.

She threw the goo on the floor and a spiral slide erupted from it with a *bang*! Neon was lifted up with it. She clung to the edge for dear life as it grew taller and taller. Up and up she went, crashing through the Goohead Central roof and into the sky, until she was cloaked in thick red clouds.

Scarlett's cackles rang out around her. Neon grimaced as her fingers began to slip.

Then the slide stopped growing and everything fell silent. Neon pulled herself on to the top and waited for Scarlett, shaking with fear.

She didn't have to wait long. Moments later, Scarlett

shot through the clouds, arms outstretched to grab her. Without a second to think, Neon pushed off and let the spiral slide take her down. Round and round she went, screaming at every bend as Scarlett clawed at her. Neon shoved a hand into her pocket and pulled out another jar.

ANGRY GRANNY SOUP GOO.

Spill for soup, the instructions read.

Neon tore off the lid and tipped it out. In a puff of smoke an angry granny appeared behind her, shouting, 'I HATE GLITTER SLIDES! Soup, anyone?'

It was enough to distract Scarlett. Neon leaned back to speed up her descent. Faster and faster she went, until she reached the ground.

'WHERE'S SCARLETT?' Moya said, racing over and helping Neon to her feet.

The angry granny goo came next, knocking Geldie over.

'She's up there,' Neon said. The room was spinning.

The whole building groaned as Scarlett smashed through the ceiling!

'And she has supervillain STRENGTH!' Geldie cried. 'The building is going to collapse!'

'Let's get out of here!' Moya yelled.

They leaped for the door, but Neon was too dizzy from the spiral slide. She stumbled and fell and landed under the half-moon table.

And then, the most extraordinary thing happened. The back of her head began to feel hot. She could feel her hair heating up. She could hear crackling.

'It can't be,' she whispered. 'Not now, surely?'

Glitter and stars and luminous green light gushed under the table and wrapped around her.

Squinting through the shimmering blizzard, she pulled her hair around to get a better look.

'GREEN!' she cried, touching the new green stripe in her hair. 'I'M A MAGICAL UNICORN! THANK YOU UNIverse! I CAN GO HO—'

A gooey hand ripped her from under the table before she could finish and hoisted her high in the air.

She dangled by one ankle, hovering over Scarlett's mouth. 'The UNIverse may have made you a magical unicorn, but I'm making you my lunch!' Scarlett said, sneering at Neon. She held up the lipstick. 'Every villain needs a wicked plan. You gave me all of it, and now finally I have become THE ULTIMATE VILLIAN! I will destroy you, and then I will destroy this world and yours!'

'And then what?' Neon cried. 'What are you going to do once you've done all that?'

'Holiday, probably,' Scarlett said, opening her mouth wider.

Through the cracks in the walls, Neon could see the street outside. Unicorns were fleeing in panic. Up above them, lightning struck the sky.

'Any last words?' Scarlett asked.

Neon tried to grab the lipstick in Scarlett's other hand, but it was too far away. She fumbled for her goo wand in her apron pocket, but Scarlett was swinging her from side to side and she couldn't reach it. She thought of home, of her parents, of the silly decoy Neon that was walking around saying, 'I like rats' – and would be doing that FOREVER if she went and got herself eaten.

A faint and familiar rumbling interrupted her thoughts. It was growing closer.

Beyond what remained of Goohead Central's walls, Neon could see a uni-taxi tearing towards her. And she could see who was driving it.

'Filly?' Neon whispered in surprise.

'That's your last word?' Scarlett said, lowering Neon ever so slightly. '*Filly?* What does that even mean?'

The uni-taxi crashed into the building, sending a gigantic wave of glitter into Scarlett's eyes.

'OWWWWWWWW!' Scarlett howled.

Neon felt herself somersaulting through the air, the lipstick flying alongside her. Scarlett had dropped them both!

The uni-taxi door was flung open.

She could see Moya and Geldie in the back seat!

She hit the ground hard, her arm outstretched to catch the lipstick.

'NOOOOOOOOOO!' Scarlett cried as she wiped the glitter from her eyes and saw what was happening.

Neon didn't waste a second – she grabbed the lipstick and dived into the uni-taxi.

She could barely breathe as they sped through the streets. Scarlett was close behind, growing larger with every roar.

'Can you go any faster?' Neon cried.

'No,' came Filly's voice over the intercom. 'But now she's made herself huge we'll be too small to keep track of. Hold on.'

The uni-taxi took a sharp right down an alleyway, then left down another. They tore through crowds of fearful unicorns running with armfuls of belongings, then across a bridge and down another alleyway, before stopping in a little garage.

WHISKERS & GLOOP DELIVERIES ONLY –
CUSTOMERS PLEASE USE THE FRONT
ENTRANCE

Filly opened the back door 'We lost her.'

All around them they could hear Scarlett's roars.

'NEON!' Moya cried, grabbing at her hair. 'You've got the streak! You're a magical unicorn like us!'

Neon pulled the lipstick from her pocket and stared at it. She could draw the portal and get out of there. She could go home – right now!

'Oh, you're not going to leave us with this mess, are you?' Filly cried.

'But I can't defeat her,' Neon said, itching to use the lipstick. 'You could all come with me and live in the human world.'

'Impossible,' Filly said. 'I would hate it, Moya wouldn't get away with half her shoe choices, and Geldie – wait, Geldie, why are you brandishing a tiny lolly stick like that'll save the world?'

He put it away sheepishly.

'Plus,' Filly went on, 'you have to stay and finish it now. You're the one who gave Scarlett her evil mission – you're her nemesis. She has to defeat you or you have to defeat her. She's not going to stop looking for you, even if you open the portal and go home. The UNIverse will be like this *forever* if you do.'

Neon thought she was probably right. But she still didn't trust her.

'Why did you come and rescue us?' she asked. 'You set me up in the Phantom Plaza so you could get the job at the Goomart, and then you cleaned up Alaric – he was my friend.'

Filly sighed. 'Not this again! I didn't set you up – you asked where the Phantom Plaza was and I told you. It's not my fault you opened a transportation goo on Scarlett Night. It's not my fault you hit Geldie in the face with a door. I was just helping Old Lady Buck. And I'm sorry for cleaning up Alaric. Everyone always talks about trying to clean him up. I didn't realise he had friends. I thought … he was like me.'

'Like you?' Neon said. 'What do you mean?'

'I don't have any friends,' Filly said. 'I try, but I always say the wrong thing, or read people's faces the wrong way. No one likes me. I just pretend I'm tough and don't care that no one likes being around me, but I'd love to have friends.'

'We can be friends!' Moya said cheerily.

'Friends,' Geldie said with a warm smile.

Neon slowly put the lipstick away. 'Friends,' she said. 'And you didn't say the wrong thing, Filly – you're right, I can't leave the UNIverse yet. And more than that, I shouldn't.'

Filly's cheeks flushed red. 'Well … I'm very rarely wrong.'

'How do you propose I defeat her?' Neon asked.

'You'll probably have to practise your goo skills,' Filly said. 'It could take years until you're up to scratch to beat a villain goo like her. You'll have to go into hiding. Train yourself up. Years of sacrifice.'

'But … I have to go home soon,' Neon said sadly.

'Does anyone have a better idea?' Filly said, looking at Moya and Geldie.

Geldie frowned, but Moya's eyes grew wide.

'I know exactly where to find a UNIverse-saving idea!' Moya cried. 'I know where we need to go!'

22

Little Trot

They drove for hours to Moya's UNIverse-saving location, which she was being very secretive about.

'It'll be a surprise, Neon!' she insisted. 'A wonderful surprise!'

Outside the taxi, zigzagging lanes stretched in every direction, surrounded by fields where luminous horses grazed on sparkly grass. The chaos of Scarlett clearly hadn't reached this part of the UNIverse yet.

Up ahead, Neon could see a yellow stone cottage with a gooey roof.

'Almost there!' Moya cheered.

Geldie looked out of the window and did a double take, then he groaned. 'No, Moya!'

'I'm surprised *you* didn't think of it, Geldie,' she said.

'Didn't think of what?' Neon asked as the uni-taxi slammed to a halt. 'Filly, do you know where we are?'

'I think so,' Filly said, rolling her eyes. 'It's *very* Moya.'

When the door to the cottage opened, Neon was surprised to see a familiar face.

'It's *you*,' she said, looking the man up and down. He was tall, with a mullet hairdo and an oversized T-shirt with a sparkly Greg-style unicorn on it.

'Have we met?' the man asked. 'Or have you just seen my face everywhere?'

'Dad, this is Neon, the human I was telling you about,' Geldie said with a sigh. 'Neon, this is my dad.'

Neon looked at Geldie in disbelief. 'Greg is YOUR DAD?! You kept that quiet!'

'*The* Greg!' Moya said, jumping from foot to foot. 'He's saved the UNIverse once and he can do it again!'

'You're the guy who made up the horse-with-a-horn thing?!' Neon cried.

'And mullets,' Greg said proudly. 'Have you heard about the mullets?'

Inside, Greg poured them all warm Volefizz, and Neon watched as the vole settled into her cup like it was a relaxing bath.

'Suzette bottles Volefizz just for me,' Greg said proudly. 'Because I saved the UNIverse.'

Greg and Geldie's house was not the kind of place Neon expected the saviour of the UNIverse to live in. It was small and cluttered, and the only thing that suggested Greg was in any way important was a framed newspaper clipping of him as a young boy, standing with the Gooheads under a headline that read:

GREG ALMIGHTY – HORSE-WITH-A-HORN
INVENTOR WE ALL THOUGHT WAS SILLY
SAVES THE UNIverse!

Neon wondered what Scarlett had done with the Gooheads. Wherever they were, they definitely weren't going to be happy with her …

'Tell me, Neon,' Greg said eagerly. 'How are the humans liking my unicorns?'

'They're a big hit,' Neon said. '*Huge.*'

Greg beamed. 'And mullets?' He ran a hand through his own.

'Um,' Neon said. 'They've … kind of gone out of fashion now, I think.'

Greg looked crestfallen. 'Oh well. You can't win them all.'

Moya finished her Volefizz and burped. 'Greg, we need to defeat Scarlett, the greatest villain goo – and for that we need the greatest unicorn mind.' She leaned forward, resting her chin on her clasped hands. 'Give us the answer. The *genius* answer.'

Greg puffed up his chest proudly. Neon was sure she saw Geldie shudder with embarrassment.

'I'm delighted you came to me,' Greg said. 'It's technically my fault Scarlett exists, but now I'm going to save the day with a great idea!'

He cracked his knuckles.

Neon leaned in closer.

'I have the solution!' he cried. 'We'll use Neon's lipstick to lock Scarlett in the human world. We'll arm her with a new evil mission to force humans to get mullet haircuts again, because quite frankly I can't understand why they've gone out of fash—'

'Nothing to do with mullets!' Filly interrupted. 'What else?'

'Well,' Greg said, pouring some more Volefizz. Even the voles were looking at him with raised eyebrows. 'How about we create an even bigger villain to defeat Scarlett. The bigger villain will eat Scarlett and the problem is solved!'

'How would we get rid of the even bigger villain that eats Scarlett?' Neon asked.

'With an *even bigger* villain,' Greg said.

'So,' Neon said slowly, 'it's like Russian dolls but with villains?'

'Exactly!' Greg said.

'Nope,' Neon said. 'That won't work. What else?'

Greg was beginning to sweat.

'We could distract her with a whole new made-up magical creature!' he said.

'Is it something with a horn?' Neon asked.

Greg sat in silence before finally muttering, '*No, it's …*' He trailed off.

Moya bounced to her feet. 'But you must have an idea, Greg!' she cheered. 'Scarlett believes she's Neon's nemesis. We've got to stop her before she destroys Neon, and the whole UNIverse!'

'But Scarlett has so many villain skills,' Geldie said quietly. 'All the evil laughs, all the fighting modes. And now, because of Neon, she finally has her evil mission – get the lipstick, destroy the UNIverse, and then the humans. Destroy *everything*.'

'Hmm,' Greg said. 'Maybe this calls for something uncomplicated. A simple battle. She's a typical villain goo – so maybe she can be lured into a typical ending. A battle of good versus evil.'

'You haven't seen the battles so far,' Moya whispered

to Greg, making a squished face and nodding in Neon's direction.

'Yes, yes,' Neon said. 'I know I'm not great at fighting Scarlett, but Greg is on to something ...'

'Ah, it's nothing,' Greg said. 'I'm just little old Greg Almighty.'

'No one calls you that, Dad, it's just you,' Geldie said.

'Me and this newspaper from a long time ago!' Greg said, pointing at the framed newspaper clipping with the Greg Almighty headline.

Neon got to her feet and began pacing. 'Maybe it *is* as simple as luring her in and cleaning her up.'

'But in your first encounter Alaric saved you, and the second time it was Filly,' Geldie pointed out. 'You might *lose*.'

'True. But,' Neon said, an idea forming, 'those battles caught me off guard, in places I don't know well. What if I take the battle to *my turf*?'

Moya clapped. 'I know where you mean!'

'Well, wherever it is, you need a faster mode of

transport,' Greg said, nodding at the uni-taxi parked outside. 'This is an end-of-UNIverse emergency.' He picked up the phone. 'Where to, Neon?'

'The Goomart,' Neon said. 'This ends in the Goomart.'

23

Airfancy

Neon stood outside the Little Trot airport. Greg was right – a plane *would* be faster!

News had spread of Scarlett's rampage and unicorns were flocking to the luminous blue building, pulling huge suitcases behind them.

'Looks like everyone's trying to get as far away from Scarlett as possible,' Geldie said.

'Great!' Moya said with absolute sincerity. 'That means the plane to Lumino will probably be empty. More airfancy snacks for us!'

'We call the planes airfancies,' Geldie informed Neon. 'I catch one every day to Lumino. They're great fun!'

As they marched inside, Neon felt wobbly with Scarlett-induced nerves, but at least the airport looked normal. It was the first time she'd felt the unicorn version and the human version were the same thing. The building was just a blue version of an airport, and the planes were no doubt the same. And that was very comforting.

Neon was very wrong.

Inside, horses manned conveyor belts of suitcases, occasionally knocking one off with their nose to check the contents and confiscate contraband.

A woman with slicked-back blue hair and a very official luminous jacket came running up and pulled an item from the horse's mouth.

'Will the person who owns this suitcase please come forward – the horse has found contraband! I know you're all panicking, but contraband will not be tolerated in ANY circumstances!'

'That's not mine!' shouted the owner of the suitcase. 'It must've crawled in there!'

Neon moved closer to see what it was.

'Caterpillars,' the woman with blue hair cried, 'are on the list of banned items.' She held the caterpillar up. 'Had this not been found, it could have been a disaster.'

Moya pointed Neon in the direction of a poster.

FOR AIRFANCY SAFETY, THE FOLLOWING
WILL BE CONSIDERED CONTRABAND BY
OUR SECURITY HORSES:

CATERPILLARS
BEETLES
BUDWORMS
SLUGS
SNAILS
RABBITS

'Huh?' Neon said. 'Why would those things be a disaster for a plane – sorry, *airfancy.*'

Moya just laughed, as if Neon was making a joke.

'No, seriously,' Neon said, trotting after the others. 'Why?'

Things became alarmingly clear after they got through security.

'Here's our ride,' Moya said.

Neon screeched to a halt.

'No!' she cried. 'We're not flying in *that,* are we?'

She had expected a colourful version of an aeroplane. But, judging by the horses at security, it was always going to be much weirder.

The airfancy was the *shape* of an aeroplane but it was completely made of goo, with a series of glowing flowers strung together where the propellers should be.

The contraband list suddenly made sense – things that would eat flower propellers.

Neon smacked a hand to her forehead. 'We're going to be kept in the air by goo and flowers?' she groaned. 'In the human world we have PROPER AEROPLANES.'

'Hardly,' said the man checking their tickets at the gate. 'I've read about them. Nothing but tin and that liquid stuff – what's it called?'

'Fuel,' Neon said.

'Well, exactly!' cried the man. 'At least flowers aren't a *liquid*. They're much sturdier!'

The airfancy had multicoloured gooey seats fitted with glow-in-the-dark seatbelts and matching armrests.

Neon took her place, between Moya and Geldie, and almost instantly the plane revved up. It sounded gruff and growly and far too angry to be powered by flower propellers.

As Moya had predicted, they were the only ones on

the flight. The only unicorns silly enough to be heading *back* to Lumino.

The plane skidded forward then left, right, left, right, left, right, left –

'Is the runway a ZIGZAG shape?!' Neon yelled, searching for something to be sick in.

'Of course,' Geldie said. 'What other shape would it be?'

Left, right, left, right and upwards!

'AAAAAAARGH!' Neon cried, as Moya, Geldie and Filly casually inspected their menus.

Being in a plane made of goo meant Neon could see everything below her feet. Admittedly, it was a little blurry, but she could make out the coloured clouds and tiny luminous horses in the fields below. It was only a matter of minutes until they were back in the red, Scarlett-struck skies.

'WELCOME TO AIRFANCY!' came a familiar voice. 'THIS IS THE FINAL FLIGHT TO LUMINO, DUE TO AN EVIL VILLIAN GOO ON THE LOOSE. IF YOU WERE UNAWARE OF THE EVIL VILLIAN GOO

WHEN BOOKING THIS FLIGHT, THEN PLEASE ENJOY SOME COMPLIMENTARY GLITTER CHUNK PLATTERS BEFORE FACING POTENTIAL DEATH.'

Neon stretched over Moya and looked down the aisle. Suzette, the squirrel made of sprinkles, was making her way towards them with a trolley!

'Goo face?' she asked, as she handed Neon a steaming blob of goo.

The second Neon accepted it, it leaped up and attached itself to her face, giving her cheeks a massage.

'What is Suzette doing here?' Neon whispered as she tried to wrestle the goo off.

'Suzette is the UNIverse's most famous entrepreneur. She invented Volefizz and airfancies, and likes to work closely with the customers and see them enjoying her creations,' Geldie whispered back.

'Oh,' Neon said. 'Just when I thought the UNIverse couldn't get any weirder. A *squirrel* entrepreneur.'

The airfancy lurched forward. They all grabbed their gooey armrests.

'What was that?' Neon fretted.

'Just red lightning,' Filly said with a yawn.

'WE'VE HIT A PATCH OF LIGHTNING,' Suzette cried, racing to the front of the cabin. 'NOTHING TO WORRY ABOU—'

The airfancy hit something hard, making everything wobble.

'That wasn't lightning!' Neon cried as one of the gooey wings went flying past the window, completely detached from the plane.

'APOLOGIES FOR THE INCONVENIENCE,' Suzette announced, as the flower propellers splatted everywhere, decorating the clouds. 'UNEXPECTED GLITTER SLIDE BY GOOHEAD CENTRAL. THIS AIRFANCY WILL NOW BEGIN AN EMERGENCY DIVE. PLEASE BRACE FOR IMPACT.'

'MY FAULT AGAIN!' Neon roared as the plane spiralled out of control.

They braced as the plane crashed straight into the roof of the Goomart. Jars of goo exploded everywhere as the plane skidded through the shelves. From the window, Neon spotted Old Lady Buck shaking her head in distress.

'WE HAVE LANDED IN THE GOOMART. APOLOGIES FOR ANY INCONVENIENCE,' Suzette announced.

'Not to worry,' Moya said, bouncing from her chair and making to disembark from what remained of the sloppy aircraft. 'The Goomart was exactly where we wanted to go!'

24

Showdown with Scarlett

Moya, Geldie, Filly and Neon sat among the Goomart chaos and waited.

Every so often, Old Lady Buck would charge past, trying in vain to clean up the thousands of spilt goos that were wreaking havoc.

'FEED ME BRAINS!' the tiny menace of a monster screamed up at Neon before charging off again.

Moya checked her unicorn watch. 'What if Scarlett doesn't come?'

'She will. Her evil plan isn't complete without this.' Neon took the lipstick from her pocket.

'What are you doing?' Geldie asked, sounding worried.

'Calling her,' Neon said, and with that she drew a line across the floor. Instantly, it began to fizz and crackle, and the others scuttled back, their mouths wide open in awe. The line became a tear and stars and glitter began to gush from the rip, flying up and out of the hole in the Goomart roof.

Through the rip, Neon could see her bedroom.

'Huh,' Filly said, sounding a bit disappointed. 'The human world is *small*.'

'That's just my bedroom,' Neon explained.

Part of her longed to jump in, for the portal to close around her so she would never have to face Scarlett.

A gust of wind blew the Goomart doors open, making everyone jump.

Neon pulled on her gloves and held the goo wand and lipstick tightly. 'She's here.'

With a blinding flash of bright red light, a blob of goo came hurtling through the door, warping and growing until it formed the familiar shape of Scarlett.

'I'm here for the lipstick,' she announced.

'You know,' Neon said, 'if this was a story, and not real life, that would sound ridiculous.'

Geldie plucked the lolly stick from his pocket and waved it threateningly.

Scarlett looked from the lolly stick to Neon and back again. 'Seriously? He's still got that thing?'

Neon didn't reply. She narrowed her eyes and raised her goo wand.

'Oh, so you're going to try to clean me up, are you?' Scarlett said, eyeing the wand. 'Well, you'll have to catch me first!'

She took off, knocking through shelves and smashing the few jars that remained intact.

'NOT THE SAUCE GOOS!' Old Lady Buck cried, as a tidal wave of condiments washed down the aisle.

Neon gave chase, leaping over out of control vines and dodging roller-skating vampires, but she couldn't keep up. Scarlett shot through a bouncy castle goo, making it pop and deflate on top of Neon.

'SHE'S GETTING AWAY!' Filly called out. 'NEON'S HIDING UNDER A BOUNCY CASTLE!'

'I'm not hiding, I'm stuck!' Neon protested.

'WE HAVE TO HELP NEON!' Neon heard

184

Moya cry. 'Help me lift this!'

She could feel Moya struggling under the weight of the deflated bouncy castle.

'I see her!' Moya cried, grabbing hold of Neon's ankle.

But then Neon felt a hand wrap around her wrist too.

'Geldie?' she asked hopefully, even though she already knew it wasn't.

Red goo pooled around her. Before she could stop it, the fingers twisted around the lipstick and pulled it from her grasp.

'NO!' Neon cried.

Moya and Geldie took hold of her ankles and yanked her out.

'GET SCARLETT!' Neon roared. 'SHE'S GOT THE LIPSTICK!'

Moya took the far-left aisle and Geldie went right. Filly stood her ground by the portal and Neon raced up the middle.

'WE CAN FLANK HER AND TRAP HER!' Neon cried.

'NO YOU CAN'T!' Scarlett squealed with delight, rising up to the ceiling.

She spun round furiously, knocking into everything and anything in her path. The others ducked.

Then she landed with a bang and raced off, emitting an eerie giggle that echoed around them. 'YOU'LL NEVER CATCH ME! YOU'LL NEVER CATCH ME!'

Neon looked up to see Old Lady Buck standing with one of the Greg unicorns from the GREGILICIOUS 3-IN-1 PICNIC GOO. She was miming a jumping move.

Neon didn't waste a second. She leaped on to the unicorn and charged in the direction of the villain goo. Scarlett was fast, but a GREGILICIOUS 3-IN-1 PICNIC GOO unicorn was faster. Neon and the unicorn soared over the shelves and came thundering back down, landing squarely on Scarlett and pinning her to the ground!

'See!' Moya said. 'Technically, Greg *was* the answer! Greg unicorns can ALWAYS save the day!'

Neon touched it with her goo wand and the unicorn

disappeared with a *pop* and a spray of glitter. She stood over Scarlett with a triumphant grin on her face.

Filly clapped and leaped about from foot to foot. 'You did it, Neon! I really didn't think you would do it!'

Next to Filly's feet, Neon could see the portal and her bedroom. She stared down at Scarlett cowering on the floor. With one flick of the goo wand the villain goo would be gone and she'd be on her way home. She'd miss her friends, but maybe she could come back and vis—

Suddenly, Scarlett grabbed her leg!

'NO!' Neon cried as what remained of the Goomart quickly turned upside down.

The villain cackled as she dangled Neon by the ankle. 'Aww, you thought you'd won. Classic mistake!'

Neon tried to hit Scarlett with the goo wand, but she was holding her at arm's length. In her other hand, Scarlett held up the lipstick in triumph.

'Put her down!' Geldie protested, brandishing his lolly stick.

'Oh, I will,' Scarlett snarled, holding Neon over the

portal. 'Time for you to fall back into the human world, my little nemesis. But we'll meet again – once I've finished destroying the UNIverse, I'll come to your world and destroy that too. Oh, I can't wait to see how you deal with me in the human world, without all your magic goos and silly goo wand.'

Neon scowled and waved the goo wand again. It was no good, she couldn't reach.

'Goodbye, Neon Gallup,' Scarlett said. 'You proved too weak to defeat the greatest villain goo in the Uni—'

'FEED ME BRAINS!' came an impatient roar, and out of the rubble burst the tiny monster. He bit down hard on Scarlett's ankle.

'OW!' she cried.

Scarlett bent forward to grab the monster.

Neon raised her goo wand.

And in one swift flick, she caught Scarlett with it.

It took the villain goo a moment to realise the wand had made contact – a moment too long. She looked up from the little monster and stared at the goo wand pressing into her arm.

The lipstick fell from her hand and rolled across the Goomart floor.

'My story is complete,' she said.

There was a crack of bright red lightning and Scarlett disappeared with a *pop*.

Neon dropped to the ground, stretching for the lipstick as she fell. But it was out of reach.

Down and down she went, tumbling through the portal.

She looked up to see her friends stretching with all their might to reach her as the rip grew smaller and smaller.

Moya, Geldie and Filly's faces grew hazier as Neon fell into her bedroom.

She bounced off her bed just as the portal vanished from sight.

The UNIverse was gone.

25

Brunty ... Forever

Neon raced downstairs and found her mum and dad in the kitchen. She threw herself across the room, giving them a huge hug.

'Neon,' her dad said quietly. 'What's happened?'

'I just wanted you to know,' she said, choking back the tears, 'I'm sorry I was grumpy and said Ratty's Cafe was silly. I really like rats now.'

'Yes,' her mum said, 'that's what you've been saying for days.'

Neon looked out of the window and saw decoy Neon disappear with a *pop*.

One Month Later

26

Chocolate Snowballs

All Neon could think about was the UNIverse.

She started wearing bright clothes again, and every night she dreamed of her friends, of Volefizz at Glittervoles and dressing up at the Slimy Wardrobe. Sometimes she dreamed of Old Lady Buck and telling her she was sorry for making such a mess of her beloved Goomart. She dreamed of cleaning it up with Geldie, racing down the aisles, armed with oversized aprons and magical goo wands. She dreamed of roller-skating vampires and of Moya and her crazy Greg-unicorn shoes. She dreamed of Alaric bounding about causing mischief and dispensing excellent shopping advice.

'We'll all have ratpuccinos, please.'

'Is she listening? Hello?'

Neon snapped out of her thoughts and forced a smile. She'd been working at Ratty's for weeks, wearing her weird furry rat-style apron and serving ratpuccinos, and the occasional ratte. The quirky cafe had become something of a bustling attraction in Brunty. People travelled for miles to dine among the lava lamps and giant cuddly toy rats.

'She's quite weird,' a girl whispered, distracting Neon from her thoughts.

Her neighbour Priscilla was there with some of her cool friends.

'Ratpuccinos coming up,' Neon said, shuffling back behind the counter.

Whenever she served Priscilla and her friends, one of them always commented that she was a bit weird.

Little did they know, only a short while ago, she'd had the weirdest life of any human on Earth.

And she missed it.

* * *

That night, Neon sat on her window sill, tracing her fingers over the little unicorn carving and wishing she could have one more day in the UNIverse.

Just then, something crackled. The room grew bright.

Neon turned slowly, not daring to get too excited. It couldn't be … could it?

A small rip snaked along her bedroom wall. Then glitter began to gush from it. Stars *pinged* around the room!

'HELLO, NEON!' came a familiar voice as Moya squeezed through the portal. 'I wore my special platforms, but I forgot my crutches!'

Neon slowly got to her feet, unable to believe her eyes.

'Moya?' she said. 'Is it really you? Are you really here?'

'Hope so,' Moya said. 'Those are very deep questions.'

'Hurry up, Moya!' came a shout from the portal. It was Filly! Next to her were Geldie and Old Lady Buck and Greg and the Gooheads!

'The Gooheads!' Neon cried. 'I'm so glad they're all right. Where were they?'

'Scarlett hid them in Whiskers & Gloop,' Moya whispered, 'in the *DANGEROUS PET GOO* section. They were not happy about it. Took us nearly a month to find them.'

Neon tried not to giggle.

'And they gave me my own portal opener!' Moya cheered. 'For helping you to save the UNIverse.'

Neon inspected Moya's portal opener. It was a box of chocolate snowballs.

'They're human chocolates, apparently. I bite into one and the white marshmallow turns colourful and shimmery and then the portal opens. The box replenishes itself too – it's an everlasting box of chocolate snowballs! And you want to know the best bit? The Gooheads have something for you too.'

'They do?' Neon said. She could feel herself getting excited. But what if it wasn't something good – what if they were furious about what she'd done to the UNIverse?

'Come on,' Moya said with a smile. 'I think you'll like it.'

27

The Deal

Back in the UNIverse, at Goohead Central, the Gooheads held a ceremony for Neon, to officially make her a unicorn – it was a lot like a school-leaving ceremony, but with less ceremony and more glitter.

'I'm enjoying your apron,' the green Goohead said, nodding at Neon's fluffy Ratty's uniform. 'You *do* like rats.'

'ATTENTION, UNICORNS,' bellowed the purple Goohead. 'Now we come to the wish portion of the day.'

'Wish?' Neon said.

'Yes,' the purple Goohead said with a rare smile. 'We would like to grant you one wish. Everyone who helped defeat the villain goo gets one wish.'

'What did you wish for?' Neon asked Moya.

'A portal opener so I could come and get you!' Moya

said, holding up the box of chocolate snowballs.

'And you?' Neon asked Geldie.

'A new helmet, with extra padding,' Geldie said, producing a very orange, very glittery, *very* padded helmet.

'And you?' Neon asked Filly.

Filly stepped forward and gestured at what seemed like thin air.

Then a ghostly tail slunk past Neon.

'Alaric?' she whispered in disbelief.

'Do you know a lot of giant ghost rats?' he asked, appearing in front of her.

'OH, ALARIC!' she cried, trying to wrap her arms around him.

'Invisible,' he said. 'Remember?'

'I wished to undo my clean-up,' Filly said with an awkward smile. 'So you could have your friend back.'

'Thank you, Filly!' Neon said, giving her a big hug. 'You could've wished for so many other things!'

'I *know* …' Filly said.

'And I bet you want to know my wish!' Greg said, stepping forward. 'I wished for mullet hairdos to become fashionable in the UNIverse!'

The Gooheads turned to reveal their new mullet hairdos.

'Our least favourite of the wishes,' the blue head said.

'And Old Lady Buck wished for her Goomart to be as good as new!' Moya said.

'FEED ME BRAINS!' cried the little monster at Neon's feet, holding up some gooey brains.

'And he finally got some brains,' Moya said. 'Not real brains, obviously, that would be disgusting.'

Neon knew what she would wish for. She squeezed her eyes shut and wished with all her might.

The purple Goohead coughed. 'You have to *tell* us,' it said. 'We're not a human birthday cake.'

'I wish I could have my portal opener back,' Neon said. 'If it's possible. That way I could visit my friends in the UNIverse.'

There was a *bang* and Neon looked down to find her battered old green lipstick nestled in her palm.

'You can be trusted,' the purple Goohead said. 'Now

that you're a unicorn, Neon, we know you will not tell our secret. And we know that you could have left the UNIverse without defeating Scarlett, but you stayed to save us all. So for that, we give you permission to travel between your world and ours. Secretly! Remember that. You must not let any humans see you.'

'I won't,' Neon said, squeezing her lipstick tightly.

'You have heard of Unicorn Hunters, I presume?' the purple Goohead said.

'Yeah,' Neon said. 'I've heard them mentioned, and Geldie told me a bit about them. They're humans who hunt unicorns?'

'Exactly,' the purple Goohead said gravely. 'They know about us, about portal openers, and they are willing to do almost anything to find us.'

Pictures of humans began to flash across the Gooheads' jars.

'There aren't too many of them left, but you must memorise their faces and avoid them at all costs. Luckily, the human world is not small – it would be unlucky if you encountered one.'

Neon nodded, but something made her freeze.

'Wait,' she said, pointing in astonishment. 'That face in the jar – it's –'

She moved closer.

It was Priscilla! Her next-door neighbour! And it wasn't just her either – she'd seen many of the faces before. The people digging by the roadside! It was most of Brunty!

Neon could feel herself sweating.

'Neon, are you OK?' Moya asked. 'You look a bit green.'

'It's a fetching shade,' the green Goohead said.

Neon was reeling.

That's what the people in Brunty had been digging for when she first arrived – a portal opener! Those T-shirts with *The UH* logo. UH stood for UNICORN HUNTERS!

'Neon, are you all right?' the

purple Goohead asked. 'Your face is doing funny things.'

Neon thought about telling them, but then they'd confiscate the lipstick and she'd never see the UNIverse or her friends again. Surely she could handle the Unicorn Hunters. They couldn't be that bad – could they?

'Neon?' the Gooheads all asked at once.

'I'M FINE!' she said, smiling sweetly. 'Everything is just *fine*.'

Back in Brunty, Neon opened the curtains of the cafe to see Priscilla standing outside, staring through the window.

'ARGH!' Neon cried. 'It's like something from a horror film when you appear like that.' She checked to make sure the lipstick was safely tucked away in her apron pocket.

'Are you open yet?' Priscilla shouted.

'Yes!' Neon called back, running to open the door

for her. She
was with
her cool friends,
including a new
one Neon hadn't
seen before.

'This is *such* a
WEIRD cafe,' he said.

Neon smiled. 'I know,'
she replied proudly, stealing
a quick glance at the
lipstick in her
pocket. 'It's very me.'

Epilogue: But ... !

Two and a half weeks later

Neon was wearing headphones and didn't hear the doorbell ring.

Downstairs, her mum let Priscilla in.

'I'm having a sleepover,' Priscilla said. 'And I saw Neon's light was on, so I thought why not come over and see if she wants to join us? She doesn't seem to have many friends yet.'

'That's a lovely idea!' Neon's mum said. 'Go on up.'

Neon had just pulled on her oversized Goomart apron and was drawing a line with her lipstick, humming along to her music. The green smudge began to rip.

There was a knock at the door, but she didn't hear it.

'Hello? Neon?' Priscilla cracked the door open.

The rip began spilling stars and glitter and luminous light into the bedroom.

'Another day in the UNIverse,' Neon said with a grin, diving through the portal.

Priscilla stood alone in Neon's room, frozen in shock. A star smacked off her cheek and bounced around the room.

She SCREAMED!

WITCH WARS

Read the whole ritzy, glitzy, witchy series!

AVAILABLE NOW!

BAD Mermaids

Read the whole fabulously fishy series!

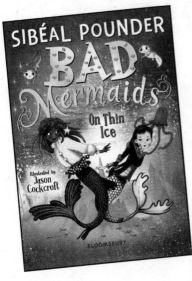

AVAILABLE NOW!

And have you read

What if somewhere along the way we've all got the Santa story a bit wrong ... ?

A funny, festive sleigh ride you'll never forget!